the christmas bet

A SWEET HOLIDAY ROMANCE

MEG EASTON

MOUNTAIN HEIGHTS
— PUBLISHING —

Cover Illustration: Alt19 Creative

Interior design: Mountain Heights Publishing

Author website: www.megeaston.com

For everyone looking for a little magic this Christmas

The Christmas Bet

one

RACHEL

RACHEL WALKED past the Christmas tree in the main area of the company offices and down the hall to the managing editor's office.

Since the door was open, she stepped in and plopped the book she'd been carrying down onto her friend Courtney's desk with a thunk, landing it right next to the figurine of Big Foot wrapped in Christmas tree lights, wearing a Santa hat. "I'm in. The bet is on."

For as much as she'd fought even reading the book in the first place, her chest was light and her heart was racing as she thought about actually committing to the bet. She'd wanted to let Court know all day, but their next magazine issue was a double, which always made their December workloads insane. She'd been scrambling all day to get the most urgent things done.

Courtney's eyes traveled from her computer screen to the book to Rachel's face before her hands got all fluttery and she picked up her desk phone. She pressed a speed dial button before putting it on speaker phone and placing the phone back into its cradle. Normally, when Courtney was behind her desk, she was the picture of professionalism—her clothes perfectly pressed, her brown hair in a bun, her expression exuding confidence, competence, and poise. But right now, she looked much more kid-at-Christmas than Managing Editor at *Memories not Dreams* magazine.

Of course, once Court stepped out of the office, she typically showed off the part of her personality that had bought the Christmas-obsessed Sasquatch sitting on her desk.

The moment Rachel heard the word "Hello?" come from the phone's speaker, she knew that Courtney had called their friend Lucy.

"Have you left for the day yet?"

"I'm in the middle of leaving—just stepped off the elevator. Why? What's up?"

Courtney looked at Rachel, excitement in her eyes. "Come back up. Rachel just said yes to the bet."

Rachel crossed her arms and rolled her eyes as Courtney ended the call. "This is not that big of a deal."

Court stood and made her way around the desk. "Yes it is, and you know it."

Okay, yeah, she knew it. Saying yes to new things was far outside Rachel's comfort zone and wasn't going to be easy. Maybe she was just saying it wasn't a big deal to make herself believe that she could do it. That it wasn't going to be so hard.

Courtney picked up the book, *A Year of Yes*, and ran a hand over the cover before meeting Rachel's eyes again. "So you read the whole thing?"

"I did." It had taken her an embarrassing amount of time to finish. Her son, Aiden, was only six, so by the time Rachel saw him after work, he was dying for her attention. As a single mom, her to-do list was always a million miles long, so it wasn't like she could just sit down and read during daytime hours. And by the time she finally fell into bed at night, she often only got a paragraph or two read before she fell asleep with the book still open.

But for a book that suggested doing something that was the very opposite of her nature, she *wanted* to do what it suggested and say yes to new experiences. On her own, though, she knew it was something she'd never convince herself to commit to, so maybe it was good that her friends were pushing her.

Lucy hurried into the office and shut the door behind her. She was panting, like she'd run the whole way, her dark bob of hair a little messier than normal, her eyes wide with excitement. "You're going to do it? I can't believe that you sat at the desk next to mine all day and didn't say anything!"

Back when Rachel was the office assistant instead of a graphic designer, she had become good friends with Lucy. It had thrilled her that she got to sit next to Lucy once she'd taken on her new job. As impossible as the task sometimes seemed as a single mom, Rachel tried to be on top of everything in her life. By contrast, Lucy was the definition of a "hot mess," which was, admittedly, rather refreshing to be around. It kept Rachel feeling balanced, somehow.

"I don't get why this is such a big deal for you two," Rachel said. She got why it was a big deal for herself— just not why her friends wanted her to do it so badly.

Courtney and Lucy shared a look before Court said, "You need everything... controlled. So this kind of thing is just a bit unusual for you."

"Oh, come on. I'm not *that* bad." Right? They didn't live in her head so they didn't really know how much she liked things organized and predictable. It couldn't be that obvious to others.

Lucy's eyebrow rose. "You sewed dividers into your purse."

"Okay, that's not controlling. That's *practical.*"

Lucy folded her arms. "And you put labeled tabs on each divider like it's a filing cabinet."

"If the three of us raced to see who could grab a

fingernail file out of their purse the quickest, who do you think would win?"

Courtney didn't even answer. She just said, "And let's not forget the Daily List on your phone."

Oof. That felt like a shot straight to the list. That thing was important and needed to be defended at all costs. "I have a lot to stay on top of. If I didn't have everything scheduled down to the minute, it wouldn't all get done."

"And then there's the Monthly Plan," Courtney said.

Lucy pointed to Courtney. "Oh, and the Yearly Plan."

"Okay," Rachel said, holding her hands up, begging them to stop before they started talking about her house cleaning list or her closet organization. She'd always loved being organized. But after what felt like a very long, grueling fight with cancer before her last scan six months ago showed no cancer, when practically everything had been out of her control, she craved being in control now more than ever.

And, okay, she had been noticing lately that it maybe wasn't always the best mindset to have, especially because she didn't want Aiden to miss out on things. Which was the only reason she was entertaining her friends' bet. "Can we get back on topic?"

"Yes," Courtney gave a single nod. "Like I mentioned when I first gave you the book—*months* ago —I think a year of saying yes to things is too much.

Baby steps are good. Are you ready to have a Christmas Season of yes?"

Rachel swallowed down her worries. "Yes."

"You don't have to say yes to the same thing more than once. This is all about trying new things and opening yourself up to new possibilities. If you try something and hate it, you're not obligated to say yes again."

Rachel nodded. That was good. She could do this.

"So you'll say yes to *everything* this Christmas?" Lucy asked like she was trying to get her to swear under oath or something.

"I mean not everything. I still have to be a responsible parent."

Courtney cocked her head. "Do you, though? Hear me out. Let's say Aiden wants dessert for dinner. Is saying yes one time going to be the worst thing ever and doom him to an adulthood of not being a productive member of society?"

Okay, okay. Perspective. That was what was going to get her through this season. Looking at the big picture. Because she wanted to say yes to more things. To live a bit more spontaneously. But she still wanted to be responsible.

"And you don't have to say yes to anything dangerous," Lucy said. "Like if a man dressed in a dark hoodie says, 'Hey, you should walk down this shadowy, sketchy alley and I'll sell you a knock-off Prada Galleria Saffiano

Double-Zip Tote Bag for fifty bucks,' you don't have to say yes to that."

"So I can say no to being ax murdered. Got it."

"And who knows?" Lucy said. "Maybe one of those yeses will bring you to the man of your dreams." She wagged her eyebrows.

That thought was laughable. "Do you really think now is the right time? When I'm so busy I can't even seem to fit in something as quick as putting in earrings in the morning?"

Lucy lifted a shoulder in a shrug. "Love is like Jell-o. There's always room for it."

Courtney clapped her hands once. "We need stakes! I can't believe we forgot the stakes. What happens if you don't follow through, and what happens if you do? We can't just have a bet for a bet's sake. There has to be consequences."

The three of them stood there in a circle—or, really, a triangle—looking at each other.

"If we were guys," Rachel said, "we would already have this part figured out."

Lucy raised a finger like she was pointing at the light bulb that just went off above her head. "I've got it! If you stick with it and say yes to everything that isn't dangerous—"

"—at least once," Court cut in.

"—then we will give you a day of pampering to die

for. If you don't, then we drive to the Wal-Mart in Littleton, go to the middle of the store, and you have to belt out Whitney Houston's *I Will Always Love You* at the top of your lungs. Deal?"

"And we get to film it," Courtney said.

Rachel bit her lip. Could she commit that fully? She really couldn't sing. At all. But that day of pampering did sound pretty glorious. And she really wanted to be more spontaneous, so maybe having something as motivation like belting out a song that no one other than Whitney Houston or Dolly Parton could pull off might be just what she needed.

Her eyes went from Courtney to Lucy, back and forth, as she tried to decide if she could. Then she tried to shake all her fears out of her head and let herself make the crazy choice. "Deal. The bet is on!"

As soon as Court's and Lucy's cheers died down a bit, she said, "And guess what the first thing is that I'm saying yes to? Getting that wreath at The Home Improvement Store that Aiden was begging me to buy. I've already called the babysitter to see if she can stay a few minutes longer."

Courtney gave Lucy a look before turning her gaze back to Rachel. "I see you're living large already."

It *was* living large. For her. She glanced down at her watch. "Oh—I've got to go! I am so behind schedule!"

※ ❄ ❄ ❄ ※

WHEN RACHEL GOT to the last stoplight before Main Street, she pulled up the Daily List on her phone. She had so much to do. Being a single parent was hard all year, but it was especially hard at Christmastime. She took a deep breath. She could be a good mom to Aiden and still get everything done.

When the light changed to green, she turned onto Main Street. It wasn't completely dark yet, but the lights that draped overhead from one side of the street to the other were on, and all the Christmas decorations in front of the shops were lit with their own lights. It reminded her that she hadn't managed to get her decorations up yet.

It was on her Monthly List, though. She had it scheduled, so it would happen.

She parked, grabbed her purse, and glanced at her watch as she speed-walked into The Home Improvement Store. Since she already knew right where the wreath was, she could just hurry to the aisle, grab one, race to the self-checkout, and she'd be pulling into her driveway not too much later than the time she'd told Bria, the sixteen-year-old who picked Aiden up from school and stayed with him until Rachel got home. Aiden was going to be so excited when she showed up with the wreath that seemed to speak to his soul.

Once she was inside the store, she turned right down the main aisle. This was no Home Depot or Lowe's— Mountain Springs wasn't big enough for that—but they sure tried to be. She passed by the aisle of electrical supplies, past plumbing, past the paint department, and then turned the corner to seasonal.

The display of wreaths with the colorful bulbs and bells sat at the end of the aisle, and a man's cart was literally caught up in them. It looked like he'd maybe turned a corner, gotten stuck on one, then the other wreaths took the opportunity to join in on the fun.

The man was good-looking, too. He was wearing a light blue polo shirt and dark wash jeans, both of which fit him extremely well. His hair was a wavy auburn and one lock curled down just above his very frustrated expression. It was actually kind of endearing, seeing him covered in Christmas like that. Maybe Lucy wasn't so off when she said that the Season of Yes could bring a man into her life. She was going to say yes to helping him out of the mess.

She headed toward him to help just as he tried to free his cart from the decorations. The rest of the display came down on him, covering him in wreaths, their bells jingling up a ruckus and causing not only everyone nearby to stop to watch, but even brought people from other aisles to see what was going on. A woman with a toddler in the cart stopped, and the toddler put both hands over his ears to block out the noise.

The poor guy's face was reddening and the harder he tried to break free from the holiday embellishments, the worse it seemed to make things. She was maybe a dozen feet from him when the man seemed to summon herculean strength and shouted "Stupid Christmas decorations!" as he threw his arms out, sending wreaths flying.

One of the wreaths came straight at her, like a missile targeted on her. She ducked, covering her face with her arms, but it still hit her right in the forehead before falling to the floor with a tinkling clatter. It hadn't hurt at all—the clanging sounded so much worse than it actually was. Bulbs clinked and bells rang, but the thing was fairly light-weight.

She picked up the wreath. It was *not* a stupid Christmas decoration, and his saying so made him so much less attractive. If she was going to meet a guy in her Season of Yes, it wasn't going to be this guy. After growing up with a dad who hated everything to do with Christmas and wouldn't let any of it into their home, she wasn't interested in a Grinch.

No matter how good he looked in that polo.

"I'm sorry," he said. He looked like he was going to

take a step toward her, but the mound of wreaths surrounding him stopped him.

She just held up the wreath and nodded. "Thanks."

Then she turned and headed toward the registers and away from the Christmas-hating man.

two

NICK

NICK WALKED out of The Home Improvement Store with barely a sliver of dignity intact. He opened his trunk, put in the gallons of primer and the bag of painter's tape, tarps, spackle, and the wreath inside, then shut it and got into his car. He couldn't believe all that happened during an innocent trip to the hardware store. He ran his hands over his face, let out a long, slow breath, then picked up his cell phone.

The background image on his phone was a picture of his wife, Clara, that he'd taken just two weeks before she'd passed away. He'd been on a business trip and just like he and Clara did every business trip, they'd video-chatted at night.

She'd already taken off her makeup and had her hair pulled up in a messy bun— something she only did in the evenings—and she had loose strands framing her face. She'd looked beautiful. He'd snapped a screenshot so he'd always have it, not knowing that it would be one of the last times he'd ever video chat with her.

Like he did whenever he felt like he needed to talk to Clara, he swiped to the last page of apps on his phone, a page with a single icon, so he could see more of her face. It kind of felt like he was actually video chatting with her, and hopefully, anyone walking by would assume he was on a video call, not just that he was talking to his dead wife.

"Hi, Clara. I'm in Mountain Springs right now, and I don't know if you've ever noticed when we've visited your parents before, but the home improvement store is actually named *The Home Improvement Store*. Those are the exact words on the building. So when you're talking to someone and say, "Bye, I'm going to the home improvement store, they don't know if you're saying it in lowercase or title caps."

He chuckled. "But since you grew up in the next town over, and I doubt that Nestled Hollow has their own home improvement store, you probably already knew that. But if that's the case, then we should've laughed about this together before now.

"I've told you that I hope that in heaven you get to watch what's going on down here like it's a TV show. If you do, I hope you were watching what just happened in there and that you were busting a gut from laughing so hard at it. Because if nothing else, I want someone to be able to laugh about it."

She probably laughed. She was probably chuckling about this conversation, too. He shook his head. "But Clara, I was kind of a jerk in there. I felt like such an uncoordinated fool, and everyone was watching and the cursed jingle bells just wouldn't stop jingling. I shouted something negative about Christmas decorations, but I'm ninety-something percent sure I didn't swear. And I should get some kind of gold star for that because I really wanted to swear—it was that bad. And then I sent a wreath flying and tagged some poor woman right in the head with it. I felt awful."

He paused for a moment and looked down Main Street at all the decorations each store had out for Christmas. Colorado Springs—where he and his six-year-old daughter, Holly, had lived until just recently—put on a pretty good display of Christmas, but nothing like Mountain Springs did. Even though Mountain Springs was probably one two-hundredth of the size, this town went all out.

He looked back at the image of Clara. "You always made Christmas so magical. I don't think I ever fully recognized all you put into it. Now that it's all my job, I realize that I have no idea how to do the same. I was at the store getting paint supplies for the new house and figured I'd just take a little stroll down the Christmas aisles to see what caught my eye. And Clara, I barely turned onto the first aisle and the decorations practically attacked me."

Now *he* was laughing at the ridiculousness of it all. He scratched his forehead with his thumb. "Anyway, I just wanted to say that I miss you. Holly misses you. Last Christmas I was still so buried in grief that I did a terrible job at making Christmas good for Holly, but I want you to know that this year, I'm going to find a way to make it magical for her. I even bought one of the wreaths after I extricated myself from them, so I've taken the first step. If you can, maybe jingle some bells near me now and then. I'll consider it you cheering me on."

He gave her one last smile, then turned off his phone and pulled out of his parking space. His last "video call" with Clara was a week ago, as he told her that he and their daughter had moved near Clara's parents as she had always hoped. Well, technically they were living *with* her parents at the moment, but the house he'd bought was just a block away.

In the week since they'd moved to Mountain Springs, he'd fixed the plumbing and some electrical issues on the new house and started cutting and installing baseboards and trim. Before long, he'd be able to paint and replace some flooring. He didn't care how hard he had to work, he would have the house ready for him and Holly to move into before Christmas.

He pulled up at his in-laws' home, which had lights on the house and trees and a manger scene out front, even though December first wasn't until tomorrow. The house he'd bought was still completely empty and didn't have a shred of Christmas decorations, so he was glad they could stay with Ben and Linda for a bit so Holly wouldn't be missing out.

When opening the door, he was immediately greeted by the smell of pot roast and... was that baking cookies? As much as he wanted to finish getting his new house ready, he couldn't deny that Linda's cooking was a huge perk of staying with them. When he got to the kitchen, Linda was at the island counter, decorating sugar cookies with Holly, and Ben was sitting at the kitchen table, reading on his tablet.

Their rough collie intercepted Nick on his way to his daughter, her long fur bouncing as she ran, then she gave a single bark, so he used both hands to scratch her head before making his way to Holly. He hugged his daughter from the side, careful not to mess with the bag of frosting in her hands. "What are you two up to?"

"Well," Holly said in her best cooking channel voice, "we decided that cookie cutters are very common, so it was up to us to use our creativity and decorate the cookies more uniquely."

It always made him chuckle when his daughter used that voice. Maybe because the words always sounded like they came from someone older than six, even if the tone didn't.

"So instead of an ordinary bulb for the circle ones, we added a marshmallow to the top of this one—doesn't he look like a melting snowman? And we decorated this one like a wreath. And see this one? We think it was supposed to be a sweater, but we turned it upside down and made it a kid throwing their arms up on Christmas morning because they're so excited."

"I love them all. Nice work, Hollybear!"

His daughter's hair was light brown, like his wife's, but it had his curls. He kept his hair fairly short, but he sometimes wondered if his would be as curly as his daughter's if it was as long as hers.

Linda slid an odd-shaped cookie—a bell, maybe?—across the counter to Holly. "Sweetie, why don't you make a surprise decoration on this one for your dad? Grandpa and I just need to talk with him for a minute. Anything goes. Make it as creative as you'd like. Just keep lassie-dog from stealing any."

"Grandma, her name is Rosy!"

Nick glanced between his in-laws. Why did he suddenly feel like he was in trouble? Nick kissed the top of Holly's head. "I'll be right back."

He followed Linda into their front room, where both

Ben and Linda took a seat in the armchairs. He suddenly didn't feel like sitting, so he just leaned against the display table in front of the window, arms folded, facing them.

Ben and Linda both looked at each other, then Ben said, "We might as well just say it. We think you should start dating again."

Nick sat up straighter, putting his hands on the table at his sides. "What?" Of all the things that ran through his mind that they might want to talk to him about, that was the furthest thing away. "Why?"

Linda leaned forward a bit, too. "I don't think that Clara knew she was going to die last fall, but she must've sensed it on some level because she mentioned a few things she wanted to have happen if she did pass away before us. One of them was you getting remarried."

Nick knew that. Clara had mentioned it to him, too. He'd laughed it off at the time, saying that it wasn't going to happen so she would just have to live forever. But Clara had said, "No, I'm serious—Holly needs a mother, even if it can't be me, and you need a wife." It had been too hard to think about, so he'd just put it out of his mind.

"Your daughter needs a mom," Linda said, echoing his thoughts of his conversation with Clara so close that it was eerie. "As time goes on, she'll need one more and more, not less."

"Are you saying that you don't think I'm doing a good enough job trying to be both parents to her?"

"That's not it at all, son," Ben said. "You're doing everything you can. That's helping. The dog is helping. We are helping."

"But there's not a whole lot that can replace a mom in a little girl's life," Linda finished.

He knew that. He did. But he loved Clara, and he couldn't imagine loving someone else like that again. "I don't think I'm ready."

"I know," Ben said. "It's hard to imagine that you'll ever be ready until you meet the one who will be your next love. You might think you can never love again, and then you'll meet your Linda." He reached across the space between the two armchairs and squeezed his wife's hand.

Nick had almost forgotten that Ben had been married before. He'd known that Ben's first wife had died in a car wreck after they'd been married only a couple of years. Before they'd had any kids. He just hadn't thought about it in a long time. But Ben was right—Nick wasn't sure he could ever love again. It just felt... weird to even try to imagine it.

"For about a year when Clara was about Holly's age," Linda said, "Ben worked overseas and only came home once a month for that full year. Now, I know it's not the same experience as having a spouse pass away, but I did often feel like I was single parenting." She paused for a long moment, then said, "and I know how lonely it got."

Her words hit him in the chest pretty hard. He felt busy all the time trying to balance work and home life. He always felt like he wasn't doing enough as Holly's only parent and as the only adult taking care of all the things they and their home needed. But as busy as he was, there still seemed to be plenty of time for him to feel those pangs of loneliness very acutely.

"You've got a fresh start here," Linda said. "You're no longer living in the home you shared with Clara, so—"

Nick shook his head. "No. Now I'm living in the home she lived in as a junior and senior in high school and with the parents who raised her."

"That's just temporary," Linda said. "You know, I can set you up with someone if you'd like."

"I am not having my *deceased wife's mom* set me up on a date."

"*I* can set you up with someone," Ben said. "A couple of guys I work with have daughters—"

"Why are you two even okay with the thought of me dating again? You should be freaking out that one day I might 'replace' your daughter."

Ben shook his head. "No one can ever replace Clara."

At least they agreed on that.

"Remember when the two of you got married?"

Linda asked. "Ben told you 'Welcome to the family,' and I said that I now consider you my son?"

Nick nodded. He'd choked up at the time.

"That didn't change just because Clara is no longer here. We still love you like a son, which means that we care about you and want what's best for you. Holly is our only grandchild, and we want what's best for her, too. You staying single forever isn't what's best for either of you."

They both kept quiet for a long moment while Nick let their words sink in. Objectively, he knew that they were right. If a friend were in his position, he would suggest the same thing. But seeing someone else go through losing a spouse and going through it yourself were two different things. He never could've guessed all the emotions that would hit him along the way.

Besides, how was he supposed to just find someone who would be okay with marriage being tied to motherhood of a six-year-old? And how was he going to find someone who was going to instantly be a great mom?

"You and Holly are all we have left," Linda said. "And we want you both to be happy."

Even though there was a wall between him and it, Nick looked in the direction of the kitchen, where he could hear the muffled sounds of a Christmas song that Holly was singing loudly, Rosy doing her best to bark backup. He always tried to do what was best for his daughter and do it all by himself. But maybe doing it all himself wasn't actually what was best for her.

And what about what was best for him? He no longer even knew what that was. He definitely didn't have that figured out.

He looked back at Linda and Ben. "Okay, I'll think about it."

Ben nodded once. "Good man. Now give me a hand and pull me up, will you?"

three

RACHEL

RACHEL OPENED her front door and called out, "I'm home!" She'd barely set her things on the small table by the door when Aiden came running down the hall toward her, their golden retriever, Bailey, hot on his heels, the babysitter close behind.

As he neared, he leaped into the air and landed on her, giving one of his patented "starfish hugs." Her son was getting bigger all the time—and faster—so she had to make sure her feet were firmly planted or he would knock her over. But after that year of being too weak for his starfish hugs, she wasn't ever going to ask him to stop.

"Hey, buddy! Guess what I got on the way home?"

He slid to the ground, so she turned and grabbed the

bag from the table and pulled out the wreath. Aiden looked at it with the same sense of wonder and admiration he'd had when they'd seen it in the store together, but this time, his expression also contained amazement at it being in their house. He ran a finger across one of the red bulbs, then turned to show it to Bria. "Isn't this the best wreath you've ever seen?"

"It sure is."

Aiden looked up at Rachel. "Can we hang it up right now?"

"Of course!" She opened the front door again, then lifted him so he could place it on the hook himself.

When she set him down, he stood back, admiring it. Then he turned his grin on her. "Thanks, momma!" Then he gave her a tight squeeze.

She didn't have a lot of money to spend on frivolous things, but this had been a good choice. Her Season of Yes was off to a good start. She grabbed her purse and the book off the table, and as they headed back toward the family room and kitchen, she said to Bria. "Thank you so much for staying later."

"No problem." Then, as Aiden raced into the family room with the dog, Bria added in a low voice, "He didn't have the best end to his school day. He was pretty upset when I picked him up."

Rachel set her things on the counter and thanked

Bria for letting her know before the girl grabbed her keys and headed out the front door. She opened the door of the fridge and looked inside as the exhaustion of the day started setting in, wishing she'd see a fully prepared meal just magically waiting for them. Maybe she would have to work some more meal prep into her Weekly Plan.

At least she had the meal planned and it was a fairly easy one. She pulled out the half of a rotisserie chicken, a package of tortillas, some grated cheese, and a jar of barbecue sauce. The barbecue sauce was key because if she used it, she could sneak in quite a few diced bell peppers without Aiden complaining, and she had a partial red one and half a green one.

As she gathered everything, Aiden told her a story about his friend, Quinton, and a small hill at school where the fields gently sloped down to the playground. "And we figured out that if we lay on our backs and lift our legs like this," he said, lifting one knee and wrapping his arms around it, "then we can slide down the hill on the snow! Did you hear that? We used our *coats* as a *sled*! It was the greatest thing ever. And then all the other kids saw us doing it and so they started doing it, too, and we basically started a new thing. I bet if we could be out there at the same time as the fourth and fifth graders, they'd be doing it, too."

Every day when she got home from work, Aiden told

her about his day at a million miles an hour, barely stopping to take a breath, and all she could do was nod and show the right facial expression. There was no space to even comment until he got enough of it out.

She dumped her armful of ingredients on the counter, then Aiden said, "Hey, can I help?"

"Always."

He stepped up on the stool, washed his hands, then scooted the stool to the counter she stood at.

As they worked and his stories paused without mentioning the end of the day, she eyed him. "How was the rest of school?"

His little shoulders dropped immediately. "Not all the way great."

That was a new thing Aiden was doing lately that she loved. Everything was related to the word "great." He was "extra great," "kind of great," and "mostly great"—how much changed, but the word "great" was always there.

"You want to tell me about it?"

He let out a huff and turned on the stool so he was facing her. "I know you told me to be nice to the mean girl because she's new and hasn't made friends yet, but she just makes me so mad!"

"Aiden, what happened?"

"I was nice to her *all* day. And she was being nice to

me, too. Then, right at the end of school, none of that even mattered. Miss Goodrich said she needs parent helpers to make the chimney and living room for our Christmas program for when we all say *The Night Before Christmas*. And momma, guess what? In class today, I only messed up on one line!"

"Good job, buddy." She gave him a high five.

"When the bell rang, I went up to my teacher and said that you could make the set."

A bolt of panic struck her. "Me?"

Aiden nodded. "I told her that you design things for your job, that you're the best at it, and that you can pretty much make anything. But Holly had gone up to talk to Miss Goodrich, too, and she said that you *weren't* the best and that her dad could do it better."

She didn't know Holly's dad at all or anything about what he could or couldn't do, but just thinking of her very full Monthly Plan made her guess he probably *could* do it better. Besides, what did she know about making set fireplaces? Not only did she not have tools for that kind of stuff, but she wouldn't have a clue of how to even start. Her design skills began and ended with digital creations.

"As sweet as it was to say all those nice things about me, honey, that seems like a really big job and will take lots of parents' help. This should probably be headed up by someone who's done this kind of thing before. Maybe Holly's dad knows what he's doing."

"Mom, did you hear what I said? She said that you weren't the best!"

She was probably right. "I know, honey. It's okay. Her dad is probably pretty good at that kind of stuff."

Aiden turned back to the roasted chicken and started pulling off chunks of meat with a little more force. "But she's trying to get him to take over everything."

Rachel pulled out the cutting board and knife and started dicing the chicken. "Holly hasn't even asked her dad about it yet, so you don't know if he even can. And honey, I don't know if *I* can. I'm working so many extra hours and trying to get ready for Christmas..."

Aiden brought his hands together, pleading. "Please, Mom? Please say yes." He hopped off his stool and went to the table to grab a paper. Then he came back and put it in her hand.

She looked down at the flyer that now had chicken fingerprints at the top and started reading about the program and how they could use volunteers. The mom guilt was getting heavier and heavier with each passing moment. But she also knew that she couldn't take on much more than she already had on her plate.

She glanced over at Aiden, who was still looking at her with hopeful eyes, the chicken in front of him all but forgotten. As she studied his expression, she tried to guess what was behind his insistence that she help. It was probably because of last Christmas. She had been going through the most intense parts of chemotherapy during the holiday season, which made her unable to do their normal traditions.

And beyond that, since she had changed job responsibilities a few months ago, she'd been working more hours to try to get her feet on the ground. Aiden was only six. He probably just wanted assurances that she would be around this year to make the season special.

But was volunteering for a project so big—a project she had very little experience with—really the right way to do it? It was such a huge commitment, and if she dropped the ball at all, it would impact a lot of people.

She glanced at her phone and could picture her Daily List and her Monthly Plan. They were already so full. The words "no," and "I'm sorry" nearly came out of her mouth.

But then she spotted the book half tucked under her purse. It hadn't even been two hours since she'd made a bet with her friends that she'd live a Season of Yes. This was exactly the kind of thing the bet was supposed to get her to say yes to.

She took a long, slow breath, and then turned to her son. "Okay, I'll tell Miss Goodrich that I'll help with it. And we'll make it awesome."

"You're the best!" Aiden said, wrapping his arms around her waist in a tight hug.

She hugged him back and smiled at him, knowing full well that she now had chicken handprints on her back.

NICK

NICK TOOK a bite of the roast beef as he watched his mother-in-law and daughter work on decorating the last few cookies. When he'd told his work that he wanted to move to Mountain Springs, they had been gracious enough to allow him to work from home four days a week. As a software developer, it was a fairly easy job to work remotely.

But they still wanted him to come in one day a week to meet with clients and his team and to coordinate with quality assurance. Those days were the hardest, because his commute was an hour in each direction on a good day, making his work day so much longer. Linda, Ben, and Holly might've already eaten when he got back from in-office days, but having a warm meal that he didn't have to prepare waiting for him when he returned was a luxury that he was going to miss when he and Holly moved into their new home in a few weeks.

"And," Holly said, dragging out the word, "done!" She held up her most recent masterpiece, which looked like Mrs. Claus with a hand up, waving. Nick was pretty sure that the cookie shape was intended to be a mitten, with Mrs. Claus's arm as the thumb.

"Nice!" Nick said. "I give this one fifty-seven stars."

Holly tilted her head. "Out of how many?"

"Fifty."

She pumped a fist. "Yes! I knew I'd get over on this one!"

As Nick walked over to the sink to rinse his plate, he asked Holly, "Want to go to the new house with me tonight to patch some holes in the walls? We can go on a hunt to find every last spot that needs fixing."

"You know it," she said before hopping down from the bar stool she'd been kneeling on. "I'll go get my stuff."

Holly was nothing if not a seeker of adventure. Of course, she was in.

Linda watched as Holly skipped out of the room, then turned to Nick. He worried for a moment that his mother-in-law was going to bring up something more about starting to date again, but instead, she said, "That will be good for her. Just so you know, she came home in a mood. The cookie decorating distracted her, but you should probably still ask about it."

Nick's attention flew to Linda as his chest tightened. "Do you know why?"

She shook her head. "Something at school. She said she would only tell you, but if I had to guess, something happened with that same boy."

THE NEW HOUSE was only a block away, but he, Holly, and Rosy still drove there. It was very cold, very dark, the sidewalks looked very slippery, and his trunk had more things than they could carry in a single load, including several gallons of primer. Besides, it was a little too chilly for the dog's paws.

When he opened his trunk, he grinned at Holly. "I know we aren't planning to decorate for Christmas until we move in, but what do you say we get a head start?" He pulled from its bag the wreath with the bulbs and bells that he'd bought and showed it to Holly.

She took the wreath in her hands, looking at it in awe. Then she ran with Rosy, the dog's yips of excitement matching Holly's, and she reached up, standing on her tippy toes, stretching her arms way up, to get it hooked on the nail that was pounded into the wooden door.

The look Holly gave him as she grinned back at where he stood by the trunk and the happiness on Rosy almost erased the bad memories of getting attacked by the blasted things in the store.

Well, maybe not *almost.* "Partially" was a better word.

Once they had all the supplies carried inside, Holly stood beside him in the family room with her hands on her hips, staring at the wall, just like he was. Except for the tools and supplies that seemed to be multiplying in the home the more days he worked on it, the place was empty and every sound they made echoed off the walls and hardwood floors.

"Okay, what we're looking for are holes like these." He stepped up to the wall and ran a finger over a nail hole, then he pulled a putty knife from the tool belt he wore. "To fix it, we just put the corner of this into the Spackle and get a little on. We only need about this much. See? Then we just push it into the hole, like this, and then lay the knife flat to scrape off the extra. Got it?"

Holly nodded, her eyebrows drawn together in serious focus.

"Okay, you try this one." He moved the step ladder just in front of a second nail hole, then handed her the putty knife. It wasn't too difficult a task for her, and based on the proud grin she gave him when the hole was no longer, she was going to love what they would be spending the next hour or so doing.

Plus, he figured it might help her get more invested in the new house and claim it as home. He was sure it wasn't easy for her to leave the home she'd spent her entire life in. He'd grown up not being exposed to home improvement stuff at all, but Clara had. Her parents were quite the DIYers, so when he and Clara had bought their first house, Clara had total confidence in picking up a saw, a hammer, a wrench, a drill, and a million other tools, and he wanted Holly to be exposed to the same thing.

He put a roll of blue painter's tape on her arm like a bracelet and told her to start filling holes and if she found anything bigger than the tip of a pencil to tear off a piece of the tape and stick it to the wall right by the hole. And then when she was finished, she could start filling the finishing nail holes in the baseboard that he'd installed yesterday.

As Holly filled a second hole that she'd found and he worked on patching a bigger hole beside the fireplace, he asked, "So, what happened at school today?"

The nice thing about Holly was that she was always willing to spill whatever was on her mind, no coaxing needed. All he had to do was open the gate.

She held up one finger as she concentrated on scraping the excess spackle from the wall, then turned around to face him, fists on her hips, getting a dab of white spackle on her pants where the putty knife in her hands bumped up against it.

After opening her mouth to speak, she closed it, then took in a deep breath. "Remember how you're always saying that it's important to help people? Especially the ones who really need it?"

He nodded slowly, wondering where this story was going that ended with her being upset.

"Well, I want you to remember that you always say that because I'm about one minute away from asking you to help my school make a living room for our program." His eyebrows rose, and Holly stayed quiet for about five seconds before saying, "Will you help make a living room for my school?"

"You want me to make you... a living room?"

"Not a real one, Dad! A fake one. With a fireplace with an opening big enough for Santa—a first-grade one — to crawl out of, with stockings hanging on it. Those can be real. And then, I don't know, a chair and a rug or something."

"Hollybear, I'm not sure I can—"

"You've got all the tools. You can use that saw you've been using for the baseboard and that other saw that's more growly and we can buy paint and I don't think it'll be too hard for us."

"I know. But there's a lot of work I've got to finish on this house so we can get moved in before Christmas."

"This is important, Dad!" Her face was so full of emotion that it surprised him.

He set down his mud pan and drywall tool then lifted her off the step stool and sat on the plastic drop cloth-covered flooring with her. "Okay, okay. Talk to me about why it's so important to you that I do it."

She gazed at the window that didn't have any blinds or curtains. With as dark as it was outside, all it showed was a reflection of the mostly empty room. Then she met his eyes. "Remember that kid I told you about?"

"The one who said he could make the best paper snowflakes?"

She nodded. "My teacher said she needed parent helpers to make the set for our Christmas program, and I was going to tell her that maybe you could help because you're fixing up an entire house. But Aiden beat me up there and he said that *his* mom would be best at it. Can you believe he said that? Like my mom couldn't do all that when she totally could have!"

"Oh, Holls," he said and pulled her in for a hug, wrapping his arms around her little shoulders. It couldn't be easy losing a mom at such a young age.

"So I told him that you'd be better at it than his mom is." Her words came out muffled against his shoulder.

He pulled back. "Holly."

"I know. I wasn't 'winning friends and influencing people,' like grandpa Ben always says I should, but *please*, Daddy. Please make the living room for us. I know it's not the same as mom doing it, but I have to show Aiden that he was wrong about her. Please?"

Nick wanted to help her. He knew he needed to do more to fill in the gaping holes left by a parent who had passed. And he wanted to do everything he could to help her not be so sad that her mom wasn't there for all of it. Could he even do this, though? Add one more thing to a long list of things to finish before Christmas?

He could. He could somehow find a way to make it all work and be awesome for his daughter when she needed him to be.

"Okay."

Holly sat up straighter, her eyebrows raised in hope. "You'll do it?"

He nodded, and she wrapped her little arms around him in a hug, which made him feel pretty great. He might not be able to give her all he wanted to, but he could give her this.

When she pulled back from the hug, she said, "I miss Mom. Can I video chat with her on your phone?"

He looked at her, confused. Holly understood that her mom was gone.

Then she gestured to the phone at his waist. "You

know, the picture you have of Mom on your phone. I've seen you talk to Mom on it."

Heat rose to his cheeks just knowing that his six-year-old caught him talking to a picture. He pulled out the phone. "You know it's not really her."

"I know. But it helps, right? It seems like it helps."

He swiped to the last page of apps and handed the phone to Holly. "I think it does."

"Hi, Momma," Holly said while looking at the screenshot, her voice full of emotion that grabbed his heart. "I miss you. We are in our new house, just fixin' things up. Check it out." She turned the phone around, so she was basically showing the picture to the walls. "And Dad's even letting me help search out all the nail holes and fill them. Mom, I'm making them practically disappear!"

She showed the picture of the tool she was using, then she turned the phone back to face her and said, "I know you're watching over us, and I think you'll really like watching us in this house. Well, I better get back to work! Love you lots and lots, Momma."

She pressed the button to turn off the screen, then handed the phone back to Nick and said, "You're right. It does help."

Holly went back to her job of filling the nail holes, this time in the baseboard, humming a tune she was probably making up. It amazed him how quickly she could bounce back from such strong emotions.

As they worked, Nick couldn't seem to get what his in-laws had said out of his mind. Now seemed as good a time as any to bring it up with Holly.

"So," he said, spreading the last of the joint compound on the hole repair, trying his best to act nonchalant, "your grandparents think I should start dating again. How do you feel about that thought?"

Holly shrugged.

"Come on. You always have an opinion about everything. What's your opinion about this?"

She was quiet for a moment, tilting her head as she slowly moved the putty knife over the baseboard. Then she turned around to face him. "Mom said you should."

"She did?" He wondered if Clara had told Holly and her parents to prepare them, just like she had with him, or if she had only gone to them after he'd brushed aside her request like it could never actually happen. Maybe she knew he'd need outside encouragement to someday date again.

Holly nodded. "She said I'd need a mom, even if it couldn't be her."

"And how do you feel about someday getting a new mom?"

"I think," she said, dragging the words out like she was trying to figure out her thoughts as she went, "that she wouldn't really be my mom, so it would be kind of weird." She bit her lip for a long moment. "But maybe it would be nice to have someone who is *like* a mom, you know? Someone else who can love me and help take care of me. It might be weird. But maybe I'd like it." She pointed the putty knife in his direction. "Only if she's nice." She waited another moment before asking, "Would it be weird for you, too?"

Holly wasn't always perceptive, but when she was, she never shied away from asking the hard questions. Questions he didn't have the answers to.

"I don't know, Hollybear. Maybe we'll just have to figure all this out as we go along."

He looked down at the gold band still on his ring finger and wondered if it was maybe time to retire it.

five
RACHEL

RACHEL PARKED in the nearest parking stall and hurried into the school. She had told Bria not to worry about picking up Aiden since she planned to be there the moment that class got out. Instead, she had to call the school to get a message to Aiden's teacher that she would be fifteen minutes late. She thought she'd be able to get off work early enough, but then a client had an issue with the layout of an ad that was super urgent, and there she was, looking irresponsible to her child's teacher.

She turned down the hallway that led to Aiden's classroom and saw him standing in the hall outside his door, arguing with a girl she could only assume was Holly. Not that they were being loud enough for her to hear what they were saying, but their rigid postures and clenched fists at their sides said that it wasn't exactly a pleasant conversation.

She hurried down the hall, but before she reached them, Miss Goodrich and a man came out of the classroom.

"Whoa," their teacher said. The woman was probably in her late thirties and for spending all day with a couple of dozen six-year-olds, was always dressed immaculately and her hair was always pulled up neatly. She was the most organized person Rachel had ever met. "What is going on here?"

The girl pointed at Aiden and said, "He's being mean" at the same time Aiden pointed at her and said, "She's being mean."

"Okay, I think you both could use a moment to cool down while I talk with your parents. Follow me."

The man stayed in the hallway, and as she neared, they met gazes. So he was the girl's dad who Aiden said was trying to "take over" the project. Somehow, she hadn't put two and two together and imagined he'd be present at this meeting to talk about the project, also. She gave him a small smile of commiseration that their kids' attentions were currently being redirected to avoid them fighting, making it feel—at least to Rachel—that she and Holly's dad were getting called to the principal's office.

As the teacher got the kids seated at desks away from

each other, working on a word search paper, Rachel tried to figure out why the man looked so familiar. She didn't have time to figure it out, though, before the teacher rejoined them in the hall.

"Rachel," Miss Goodrich said, "this is Nick Stewart, Holly's dad. Nick, this is Rachel Meadows, Aiden's mom."

She suddenly realized why the man—Nick—looked familiar. He was the guy trapped in the Christmas wreaths at The Home Improvement Store. *Great.* She would be working on a Christmas set piece with a Christmas hater.

Nick looked like he was about her age, fairly tall, nice build. He had auburn hair that was long enough on top that it showed that it had a slight curl. It was a color she didn't see often on a man but went so well with his skin tone. And his eyes were striking. They were the color of the sea on a cloudy day, with a rim of darker blue, leaning toward teal. And right now, she was seeing the concern in them.

Miss Goodrich brought her hands together in front of her. "You probably already know that your kids aren't getting along with each other so well."

Rachel nodded.

"I've been worried that Holly isn't making new friends," Holly's dad said. "I thought kids forgave each other like two seconds after a disagreement and then were practically inseparable."

Miss Goodrich lifted one shoulder in the slightest shrug. "And maybe they'll get to that point. But I think other issues are going on that's stopping that."

Rachel could guess what Aiden's issues were. And they were probably all related to it being Christmastime and the fact that she was so sick from the cancer and treatments last Christmas.

"I've pulled them aside separately to try to get to the bottom of the issue. There might be multiple issues, but it seems like the big one is jealousy. And a bit of insecurity."

Rachel's eyebrows shot up and she pulled back in surprise. Nick's reaction mirrored hers. "Jealousy?"

"I hope I'm not offending either of you by saying this, but I do think you need to know." She turned to Rachel. "Aiden doesn't have a dad, right? He isn't in his life?"

Heat crept up Rachel's neck and she hoped she wasn't blushing. It was just a fact. A fact that rarely embarrassed her. But she normally wasn't in the position of talking with a teacher about an issue with her usually sweet, thoughtful son and getting called out on it.

She cleared her throat. "No. He never has been."

She was pretty sure that Nick just stole a glance at her ring finger.

Miss Goodrich held out a hand like she was presenting Nick. "And Holly has a dad who's always there for her."

The revelation shocked her even more than the jealousy comment did. Aiden's dad had never been in the picture. Aiden did have an uncle who he loved and who was great with him, though. She had always promised her son that she would find him a dad someday, but he had never even mentioned being sad that he didn't have one. Between that and the fact that Rachel had grown up with a dad who wasn't the nicest guy even when he wasn't drunk, it had somehow never occurred to her that Aiden would feel that loss.

Yet Rachel knew that dads were important and made a big difference in a child's life. She knew he needed one, but she hadn't realized he had gotten to the age where it had become so important.

She *did* want to find someone and get married. She *did* want him to have a dad. But like so many things as a single mom, it just never really fit into her plans.

Miss Goodrich turned to Nick. "Holly's mom passed away, right?"

Rachel sucked in a breath as a pang of sadness hit her. She found herself glancing at Nick's ring finger and the gold band that was there. He seemed to sense Rachel's gaze on it because he twisted it around his finger somewhat self-consciously before he pushed his hands into the pockets of his pants.

"Yes. Just before Thanksgiving last year."

Miss Goodrich gestured to Rachel. "And Aiden has a mom who does everything with him."

Nick shot Rachel a glance before looking back at the teacher. "You really think that's why they've been fighting so much?"

She nodded. "I do. I'll keep helping all I can at school, but I just wanted you two to be aware in case opportunities come up at home where you can discuss it with your child."

Both she and Nick nodded. She wondered if his head was as full as hers was right now.

"Now come in," Miss Goodrich said as she waved them into the classroom, "I got both of your papers saying you are willing to help with the set, so let's talk about the project."

Aiden and Holly joined the three of them at the table in the back of the room, and Miss Goodrich talked about their Christmas program. Rachel kept glancing at her son, trying to guess what was going on in his head, and had to force herself to focus on what his teacher was saying.

Miss Goodrich said that several parents had filled out the request for help form. Parents had offered a padded armchair and a rug for their stage living room, and some parents donated cash, so they should have enough for the supplies they needed to make the fireplace.

"Neither of you has a Santa costume that will fit a six-year-old, do you?"

She and Nick both shook their heads.

"That's okay; we'll get that taken care of. So all we need the two of you to do is to make a fireplace and chimney about four feet wide and about eight feet tall."

Rachel gave Nick a smile, mentally crossing all her fingers that this guy knew the first thing about making a large fake fireplace because she sure didn't.

APPARENTLY, what they needed was to have all four of them go to The Home Improvement Store and get a four-by-eight-foot piece of plywood and several two-by-fours, which Nick arranged with the store to have delivered to his house before the four of them set off to shop for the other supplies. Aiden and Holly wanted a brick fireplace, and they found some 3-D Styrofoam brick panels that looked like real brick and were lightweight enough that they wouldn't make the project unmanageably heavy.

"Okay, construction adhesive..." Nick said after he turned the cart onto an aisle with dozens of options. Rachel scanned the columns of products, trying to land her eyes on anything that said construction adhesive but finding nothing.

Holly picked one up, her eyebrows drawn together, and looked at her dad. "This is caulking, right?"

"What's caulking?" Aiden asked, tripping over the unfamiliar word.

Holly turned to him. "After you put in the base-boards, you squirt a line of this along the top of it and smooth it out all pretty. It makes that little space disappear."

Aiden turned to Rachel. "Disappear?"

"Not disappear," Rachel said. "It just hides it."

"Some of these are just used for one thing," Nick told both kids. "Glue or caulking. But some, like these over here, can be used for both."

Rachel just watched as Nick, crouched down on the balls of his feet, answered all of both kids' questions. He answered so patiently, too, even though the kids seemed to be in a competition for who could ask the most questions. And she watched Aiden's face as he ate up every single word that Nick said. Aiden hadn't even shown any kind of interest in home improvement or construction-type stuff before, so it wasn't like he finally had someone to answer his questions.

But who knew? Maybe he hadn't shown any interest because he hadn't been exposed to it before. He did enjoy doing crafty things—maybe this was just a bigger version of that passion. Or maybe he was just showing interest because Miss Goodrich had been right in guessing that Aiden wanted a dad in his life.

She tried to think back to her second impression of Nick—she'd already decided that she was going to pretend the first impression with the wreaths hadn't happened—when she'd hurried down the hall to where Aiden and Holly were arguing earlier. Had she noticed then just how attractive he was?

Yeah, she'd noticed. So maybe it was how adorable he was, crouched down and talking with her son that made her heartstrings stand up and take notice. This was her Season of Yes. She should say yes to being attracted to this man. It was practically part of the bet, right?

The man grabbed two tubes of what must be construction adhesive and tossed them into the cart with the panels and some screws they'd added along the way. Rachel took the break in conversation to ask what she'd been wondering on and off for most of the shopping trip. "What do you do for a living?"

"I'm a computer programmer. I help make the software used for many online courses."

"Software? I assumed you worked in construction." Especially because the first time she'd seen him, he'd been at a hardware store.

He laughed. It was a nice sound—the kind that made her chest feel instantly lighter. "No. Don't mistake my ability to explain caulking to a couple of six-year-olds for expertise. I know just enough to be dangerous."

"You're not dangerous, Daddy," Holly said, walking alongside the cart with one hand on it. She looked at Rachel. "He's not—he's really careful. We got a new house and he's redoing everything in it. It'll be all done just in time for Christmas."

Rachel raised an eyebrow. "It sounds like you know a lot about this stuff."

"My dad was in the military," Nick said. "And although we lived on plenty of bases all over the world that really could've used some home improvement, we never did any ourselves. But my in-laws practically built the house they live in, so my wife, Clara, grew up helping with every project imaginable. When we bought our first home—a place that had seen better days—Clara and I did all the work of fixing it up ourselves. I learned as I went."

He glanced down at his wedding ring, seeming... uncomfortable, was it? Self-conscious? Rachel couldn't quite tell. Either way, this was clearly a guy who was still grieving, and Season of Yes or not, she had no business checking out how nicely those shoulder muscles filled out his t-shirt.

"Look, Dad!" Holly said, pointing. "The wreaths! Let's turn down that aisle."

Nick chuckled as he rubbed the back of his neck.

"Uh, that aisle is dangerous to take a cart down." He shot a glance at Rachel. "Sorry for the other day, by the way."

She hadn't realized that he'd recognized her from that brief interaction. She figured his mind had only been on freeing himself from the wreaths. They were all hanging nicely on their hooks now. "I'm glad to see you and the wreaths both made it out of the tussle unscathed."

"Well, I wouldn't say *entirely* unscathed. My ego left here looking like it had been in a fight with an alley cat."

The expression on his face was adorable, and she couldn't stop looking into those striking eyes.

Nick cleared his throat. "So, when are you free to start working on this?"

Rachel opened the flap of her purse as they walked and pulled out the planner from the "records" tab. She glanced through the things they had coming up—and there were a lot of them—and only saw one opening over the next few days. "We are available tomorrow."

Holly put her hands together, pleading. "Aiden has a dog."

"Bailey," Aiden said.

"Can they please bring her, too? Then Rosy will have someone to play with."

Nick looked at Rachel and she nodded, so he told Holly yes. Then he scratched down his address on the note paper they'd been using as a shopping list and handed it to her. "Tomorrow it is."

Okay, tomorrow. She wrote it down in her planner. And since he was right next to her, she didn't write down what she knew she should—a reminder to not notice how attractive he was or what a good dad he was.

Of course, that ring on his finger was its own reminder that he was every bit as unavailable as if he was actually married.

six

NICK

NICK SANK onto his bed and adjusted the pillow against the headboard so he could sit up comfortably. It had been such a long day, and he was exhausted. But Clara's parents had gone to bed and Holly was asleep and he was finally able to crash in this temporary room of his. He opened his phone and flipped to the last page of apps so he could see Clara's picture and smiled back at her.

"Remember that conversation you had with me a month or so before you passed away where you said that if you ever died that I should remarry quickly so I wouldn't be alone and so that Holly would have a mom?" He gazed up at where the corner of his room met the ceiling for a moment before looking back at the phone. "I'm sorry I completely blew you off at the time.

You probably needed me to say that I understood instead of just saying that your death wasn't ever going to happen.

"I like to think that you had the same conversation with Holly and with your parents to prepare them, too, because that's the kind of thing you would do. If part of the reason why you told them was because I had ignored your plea, I apologize." He shook his head. "But between your parents, Holly, and Holly's teacher, I got your message loud and clear this week."

He shifted the way he was holding the phone so he could pull his wedding ring off his finger. Then he held it up between his thumb and pointer finger and just looked at it for a long moment.

He shifted his gaze back to the phone. "I think maybe it's time I stop wearing this. Actually, today it felt like it was time to stop quite a while ago, and I've probably been ignoring that, too. I'm hoping that seeing me take this off and taking the first step to moving on is making you cheer. I mean, in a way, it feels good to be making this step finally."

He paused for a long moment, not sure what to say. "At the same time, though, I don't know how I feel about it. I can definitely say there's not any cheering going on over here." He shrugged. "But somehow, it also feels right, if that makes any kind of sense. Even though I know this is what you wanted, it's still hard. Just know that I'll never stop loving you, okay?"

He twisted in the bed to pull open the drawer of his nightstand and placed the ring inside before pushing it closed.

"Goodnight, Clara." He turned off his phone and the lamp before readjusting the pillow and lying down, staring up into the darkness, praying that he could make it through everything that lay ahead of him.

NICK WAS glad that today had been a remote work day instead of one where he had to drive to the office. The day had been full of both meetings and deep focus work, but it meant that he was able to finish early enough for him and Holly to grab a bite of dinner before heading over to their new house with Holly's dog, Rosy.

When he heard the knock on his new door, he answered it, letting in a gust of freezing wind blowing with it the powdery snowflakes that covered everything. Rachel, Aiden, and their golden retriever were all shivering in the light of the porch, so he said, "Come in, come in."

"Hey," Aiden said, "you've got the same wreath on your door that we have on ours!"

Aiden shrugged out of his coat and handed it to his

mom, then he and their dog raced through the foyer and into the big kitchen, dining room, and family room where Rosy was barking her own hello.

"Welcome to our home that we don't even live in yet," Nick said. It felt weird to welcome guests into a home with no furniture—just empty, echoing spaces. He didn't have a coat rack or even a chair to put their coats on, so he added Rachel's and Aiden's coats to his and Holly's on the railing leading to the upstairs.

Rachel looked all around the area. "I love what you've done with the place."

"I've heard that a minimalist look combined with sawdust and accents of construction tools is what's in this season."

"I work at a magazine, so I've got some contacts. I think I'll have to put in a call to see if we can get HGTV Magazine to come spotlight the look."

He chuckled. "I've been told that I have the magic touch when it comes to home decor."

"I can tell by the wreath you chose for your front door."

His face immediately heated just thinking of their first interaction, before he'd known who she was and when he'd been trapped under an avalanche of the things. Luckily, though, she wasn't looking at his face. She put her hand on the trim that went around the opening into the living room. It hadn't had any until a couple of days ago. It still wasn't painted, but all the nail holes were filled and sanded and everything was caulked.

"Seriously, though, this looks incredible." she walked into the living room, glancing around at all the work he'd done. "You learned all this just by trial and error?"

"Well, in all fairness, the bulk of the errors happened at the previous house." The kids and the dogs were both racing around the open spaces. They sounded happy and occupied, so he asked, "Would you like the grand tour?"

Rachel appeared interested in the idea, so he took her up the stairs first. Maybe because he was eating up her praise and he'd put in a lot of work on that staircase and railing. As she looked around at the room that would be Holly's once they moved in, he said, "It's good to see you again when I'm not trapped under a mountain of Christmas decorations or when we aren't being called out by a teacher."

"Neither of us got after-school detention, so I say we call it a win."

He smiled at her. It had been a very long time since he'd last flirt-bantered. It was nice to know he could still do it, even if he was a little rusty.

The sounds coming from downstairs seemed to instantly turn argumentative, so they hurried back to the family room. Holly and Aiden were having a heated discussion about which parent was more creative.

"Whoa," he said. "Why am I hearing so many angry voices?"

Aiden turned to Rachel. "She said that since we are making the fireplace here, it means that her dad won. That he's the best at this kind of stuff."

Nick was so embarrassed that Holly was acting like she was. He loved that she had a spitfire personality. At least most of the time. He didn't love seeing it aimed negatively at others. He was going to have to have a good discussion with her about this later.

"I was just defending your honor, Dad."

"Hollybear, my honor doesn't need to be defended. Our guests *do* need to feel welcomed, though. How do you think you can help with that?"

"Are you trying to be grandpa, Daddy? Because sometimes 'winning friends and influencing people' doesn't feel like the most important thing. Letting someone know when they're wrong is."

"Holly!"

She took a deep breath and blew it out slowly. "You're right. Now isn't the time to point out that Miss Goodrich says she tells us when we got the wrong answer because that's how we learn. Now's the time to work together."

He rubbed a hand across his forehead. It was at times like this he wished Clara was still there. They could figure out how to help Holly together, instead of him trying to figure it all out by himself and constantly worrying that he was doing it wrong. He wanted to pull her aside right now and talk to her about everything. But he also didn't want to make the situation more awkward than it already was for Rachel and Aiden.

Before he could even open his mouth, though, Holly turned to Aiden. "I'm sorry for what I said."

Aiden tapped a finger on his lip, then smiled and said, "Thanks. Me, too."

Holly may be a spitfire, but she was always quick to apologize. He'd never been so grateful for that trait of hers.

Quickly after, Rachel got both kids turned around and looking down at the plywood. It lay right in the middle of the mostly open space. Since this was the biggest room in the house and most central, it was where he kept all of his construction supplies and tools, but he mostly had them on a tarp near the wall by the fireplace and out of the way.

"So," Rachel said, "the fireplace is at the bottom, with the mantle about halfway up, right?"

Aiden nodded. "Yep! And we need to cut open the middle part because a kid in our class"—

"Zach S."—Holly cut in.

"—is going to be Santa Claus, and he needs to come from behind it, like he came down the chimney."

Rachel grabbed the tape measure from his supplies

and sat down on the floor with her legs crossed. "Well, then, it sounds like we need to figure out how tall that opening needs to be for Santa to climb out of it." She extended the tape a good three feet, then held it measuring from the floor up, and had both kids walk beside it, crouched, so she could measure.

Since the wood they were working with was only four feet wide, the logical width of the opening was two or two and a half feet wide, and if they were doing the mantle halfway up, the logical height of the opening was about three feet high. That would leave enough space to do the faux bricks surrounding it.

They could've figured that out even if the kids weren't present. But Rachel was telling them how many inches high they were as they crouched past the tape, and both of them were going past it time and time again, trying to get lower, the dogs participating right along with them, the kids' laughter building with each pass.

The sound made his heart happy in a way he hadn't felt lately. Like a tiny little piece of it was fused back into place.

No, it was more than that. The more he watched, the more he realized the feeling came from knowing a piece of *Holly's* heart was fusing back into place. He knew that leaving their old home was the right choice and that Holly was excited to move close to her grandparents. It was still hard, though. It was the only home she'd ever known. It was where her friends were, and she was apprehensive about making new friends.

But he'd assured her that she would. Every day after school over the past two weeks since they'd moved to Mountain Springs, he'd ask if she'd made any friends that day. The only kid he ever heard about was Aiden and how much they *weren't* becoming friends. Finding out from Holly's teacher that she was struggling because Clara was gone had just pulled at his already frayed heart.

He studied Rachel as the kids and the dogs went around and around. The smile on her face was open. Full of Joy. Her green eyes sparkled and her dark hair fell in big waves down to her shoulders, framing her face. Watching her help the kids turn from anger to happiness was mesmerizing. *She* was mesmerizing.

Eventually, the kids fell to the floor, exhausted from laughing, but they still managed to laugh and squirm more once the dogs started licking their faces. Rachel turned to him and grinned. "I think three feet will do it."

"Thank you," he said, and it was the most genuine *thank you* he'd given in a long time.

She smiled back at him, and he had to admit it did something to his stomach. Something rather unexpected.

He and Rachel lifted the piece of plywood onto two saw horses, putting it closer to waist height, and she measured the wood three feet from the bottom in a couple of places, marking each. He placed his framing square against the side of the plywood so he could make sure the line they were making would be perfectly parallel to the base. Then he held it down with his left hand so he could mark the line with his right.

As soon as he put his hand on the square, his ring looked conspicuously absent. At first, he thought that maybe it just looked that way to him, since he'd spent the last nearly eight years always seeing it there, but Rachel seemed to notice every bit as much.

Enough that it felt like a tangible thing in the air between them, begging for a comment from him. He cleared his throat. "It was time." He watched as the expression on Rachel's face changed, but as much as he studied it, he couldn't guess what she might be thinking.

He hadn't noticed what Holly was doing, since she was on the floor behind him, playing with the dogs, but she'd apparently had a great vantage point for witnessing the exchange. She reached forward and patted him on the leg.

The perceptive kid had noticed the lack of his ring within moments of seeing him this morning. He'd told her that it was hard to take it off, but that he knew he should. She'd said, "It doesn't mean you don't love Mommy still. It just means that you know she's in heaven, and we need to keep on living here." He'd been worried about telling her, yet she'd been the one to share wisdom and reassurance with him.

Sometimes it felt like Holly had the insight of someone well beyond her years, then she would show the maturity of someone exactly her age when she played the whole "my dad can beat up your dad" card with Aiden. The girl was a walking dichotomy, and he loved her fiercely.

Before long, he and Rachel had the opening cut. Pretty quickly after that, they'd figured out how to use the two-by-fours to construct a frame on the back of the fireplace to make it freestanding. They'd even had enough wood left over to create the mantle and get it screwed to the plywood. And it had all generated enough small leftover pieces of the two-by-fours that the kids were having a blast using them like building blocks.

It had taken a lot of back-and-forth discussion and lots of measuring and math to decide how to make the piece. He and Rachel stood next to each other, grinning at the very plain fireplace. Both Holly and Aiden crouched down and climbed through the fireplace opening, just to test it.

Rachel turned to him. "We did good work."

His smile was big as he nodded. "We did."

Before they started, he'd wished that Clara was there to help him figure it all out, because she'd always been crafty. But what he'd experienced that evening with

Rachel had been rather remarkable. Neither of them had known what they were doing when they started, but together, they figured it out just fine and the results were pretty great. *Everything* he was feeling was pretty great. It was nice to experience that specific sense of teamwork again that could only come when two people figured things out together.

The kids were now playing something with the extra wood pieces that seemed to be a mix of the floor is lava and follow the leader, all while chanting the lines of *The Night Before Christmas* that they'd memorized.

He turned to Rachel, hoping that he could manage to take a leap of faith without crashing and burning at takeoff. "Holly and I have a few Christmas traditions of going to holiday outings, but most of them were tied to our old town. Well, except for my in-laws' ugly sweater party. We've got a fresh start here, and we decided that we need a few new traditions. Do you have any suggestions?"

He wasn't asking Rachel on a date. The last time he'd asked someone on a first date was ten years ago, and he wasn't quite ready to take a leap that big. But he also knew that it would only take about one more day to finish the fireplace, and he wanted to see Rachel again.

Rachel's entire face had brightened when he mentioned Christmas traditions, but then she seemed to hesitate. He held his breath as he waited for her response. It was fine if she just recommended a town event that he and Holly could attend or told him about a Christmas activity. He hoped that she would take it as an opening to see each other again.

She bit her lip and looked at Aiden, thinking. Not thinking, like she was coming up with a list of things to suggest, but thinking like she was trying to decide something. She clearly understood that his question was an opening.

He continued holding his breath.

Then she turned back to him. "Yes."

"Yes?" He wasn't quite sure what that meant.

"The snow sculpture activity in Downtown Park happened last week, but they're still there. And there's Santa's village, a manger scene, a gingerbread house with hot chocolate, the works. Aiden and I planned to go tomorrow. Would you like to join us?" Her expression was uncertain, but he could see the hope behind it, too.

He grinned. "We'd love to."

seven

RACHEL

RACHEL WAS JUST SAVING all of her work in Photoshop, Illustrator, and InDesign—yes, she'd managed to use all three today—and closing out of her many open tabs in her browser when her desk phone rang. A second phone started ringing on Lucy's desk in their shared cubicle. They both picked them up and said hello at the same time.

"I'm so glad I was able to catch you both," Courtney said in her professional, *I'm on the clock* voice. "It is Wednesday, which means it's been one full week since the bet officially started and we need to do a check-in. Will you both please meet me in my office promptly at five o'clock?"

Rachel glanced at the clock at the bottom of her computer screen. That gave her five minutes to wrap up.

"Yep. For once, I'm actually finished with everything on time."

She glanced at Lucy, whose eyes were on her screen in a frantic focus and whose desk was a mess of printed magazine layouts, sketches, post-it notes, and a half-eaten bag of peppermint bark. "I'm not finished, but I can come back... Do you know what?" She leaned back in her chair. "This all can wait until tomorrow. See you at five!"

They both hung up and Rachel organized the few papers she had on her desk and put some items into tomorrow's Daily List on her phone. Then she and Lucy headed to Courtney's office.

Court was focused on something on her iPad, but she glanced up long enough to wave them in and say, "Take a seat."

And then, like Courtney's internal clock knew right when the work day ended, she turned off the iPad screen, set down the pencil, and grinned at Rachel. "Okay, it's been a week since we made our bet, and L and I want an update. Will we be pampering experiencing a concert put on only by you?"

Lucy rubbed her hands together. "We everything you said yes to."

"And if you said no to anything "

Rachel took a deep breath, '
the past week. They had texted in

times that they had already been updated on much of it, so she tried to think of the things she hadn't already shared. She probably should've been keeping a list on her phone.

"I think Aiden's onto me. So far, he's asked for a later bedtime, to put a tree he made out of Legos as the topper on our Christmas tree—yes, we have a tree on top of our tree now—to skip doing his reading homework one night, and to wear all of his clothes inside out to school one day. I think my saying yes to that one was what tipped him off. He learned pretty quickly not to ask for the same thing twice."

"He never asked for ice cream for dinner?" Courtney asked. "Such a shame."

"No, but he did talk me into getting ice cream and eating it outside in the snow. I think I still have a touch of frostbite on my lips." She touched her lips and for some crazy reason, Nick popped into her mind.

"And you said yes to everything?" Lucy asked.

"Yep."

"Okay," Courtney said, "but that's saying yes to Aiden, which wasn't exactly the point. What else did you say yes to?"

"I already told you that I said yes to helping with [Aid]en's class Christmas program and that I said yes to [build]ing a four-foot by eight-foot fireplace to use as a set [piece.] They still looked impressed by that one, which they should be since she had never done anything like that before. "Oh, and I think I said yes to a date tonight."

"What?" Courtney said, getting out of her chair behind the desk and coming around to sit on the edge of the desk in front of Rachel, right as Lucy said, "For real?"

"Okay, you don't need to act so shocked. Plus, it's not really a date."

Courtney folded her arms. "Explain."

"I'm working with the dad of one of Aiden's classmates on that fireplace, and we are getting together with our kids."

"Divorced?" Courtney asked.

"No. Widowed."

"Oh! A single dad!" Lucy said. "My heart just melted like snow on a warm spring day."

"I don't know," Rachel said, fiddling with a piece of lint that was on her skirt. "His wife passed away more than a year ago, but up until a couple of days ago, he was still wearing a wedding ring." She looked at her friends. "Do you think that's a bad sign?"

Courtney cocked her head. "I think that's the sign of a guy with the capacity to love someone deeply. Where are you going?"

"To Downtown Park to see the snow sculptures and Christmas village."

Lucy wagged her eyebrows. "I heard that if you both

wear Santa hats when you walk under the arch to the train that goes around Santa's village, you'll fall in love."

Rachel chuckled, shaking her head. "Yeah...My six-year-old told me the same thing. He also believes in Santa Claus."

TONIGHT, Rachel said yes to Aiden wearing his Santa hat to the park. But because she also didn't want her kid to freeze to death, she said yes to him wearing it on top of a knit hat that would actually keep his adorable head warm.

As they got out of the car and walked to where they could see Nick and Holly waiting by the manger scene, she laughed out loud when she saw Nick's hat—it was knit, like all of theirs were, but his was red with fluffy white around the base and a white pom on top. She loved that Christmas was in his heart enough to do something like choosing to wear a knit Santa hat in public. A lot of guys might have been embarrassed. She wondered if he had any idea how attractive it made him.

Not that the guy needed any help in that department. He even looked attractive in a winter coat and boots. And the fact that he was holding his little girl's hand made her heart get a little melty, too.

"Hi," she said as they reached them, not meaning for

her voice to come out nearly as breathy as it did. Maybe that was a side effect of a melting heart. She cleared her throat like maybe it was the cold or something that had caused it, but by the way the corner of Nick's mouth pulled up just a bit, he didn't buy it. "Should we go check out the snow sculptures?"

They had only looked at a single sculpture together —a couple of carolers—before Aiden and Holly ran to the next one. It was a giant Santa head and shoulders as if he was a mythical beast rising out of the ground. As the kids raced on to one that looked like it was probably supposed to be Snoopy lying on top of his dog house, Rachel said, "We might think we've lost them for a bit, but I'm betting they'll come back to pull us to look at a dozen different sculptures before we're done."

Nick laughed as they meandered through the sculptures filling the open area of the park. "I expect nothing less."

Nick stopped walking to watch their kids gaze in wonder at a sculpture that looked like a miniature log cabin with Santa at the chimney, so she took the moment to sneak a peek at him. Those striking eyes of his were crinkled at the sides from smiling and he looked so thrilled that the two kids were getting along. At least, they were for that exact moment.

She noticed his hat again and was suddenly very curious about his childhood. As they started walking through the sculptures again in the same direction the kids were heading, she asked, "What was Christmas like for you growing up?"

He looked up a bit and gave a slight shrug. "Pretty typical, I guess. Tree, stockings, a special dinner, a present we could open on Christmas Eve that was always pajamas, presents Christmas morning."

Everything she had craved as a child. "I need to hear more about the Christmas Eve pajamas. Matching or not?"

He chuckled and scratched at the stubble on his jaw. "Always one piece—the kind with feet that zips up. And always matching for all of us, my parents included. For as many people who have the Christmas Eve pajamas tradition, ours was probably a bit more unique just because of the fabric.

"One year, it was reindeer. And I'm not talking pictures of reindeer on the fabric, I mean it was like a reindeer costume. There was even a hood with antlers. Another year, there were these green fringe pieces hanging down that made us look like Christmas trees. One year, it was elves, another, gingerbread men."

He chuckled again. "One time, it was the words 'You'll shoot your eye out,' with a pair of glasses as the O's, you know, from A Christmas Story. My dad loved that movie. There was a flap in the back of those pajamas. Oh, and one year, they were covered in Christmas lights that glowed in the dark. I think it prepared me for my future in-laws' ugly sweater party."

She was trying not to listen with her mouth dropped open in awe and longing. "Your family sounds fun. Do you see them often?"

He shook his head. "Not nearly as often as I'd like. Since my dad was in the military and we moved all around, it kind of gave everyone wanderlust. We are spread all over the world now, so we only get together during the summer every other year." He glanced over at her as they stopped to watch the kids check out a snow sculpture of a man sitting on the actual park bench. "Have you moved much?"

"No. My wanderlust is limited to travel, which I guess is to be expected when you work for a travel magazine. We've lived in Mountain Springs since Aiden was a year old."

"So you didn't grow up with all this?" He motioned to the entirety of everything in the park.

"Nope. I grew up in Erie."

"And what was Christmas like for you? What kind of traditions did you have?"

She shrugged. "We only had one. Well, two, kind of. The second was because of the first. My dad hated Christmas, so we couldn't celebrate it at all unless we wanted him to be even more cranky than usual, and he was very cranky about everything at Christmastime. He probably had his own trauma related to the holiday, but it wasn't like I was going to ask about it.

"My mom had no issue with the holiday, but she reacted to my dad's 'seasonal irritability' by kind of checking out. When she was present, she would leave a Dove chocolate on my pillow. It wasn't Christmassy, so we didn't risk setting off my dad, but the first time she gave me one, she told me that doves represent peace, so it was my little piece of peace for when our house wasn't peaceful. I lived for getting those little chocolates on my pillow."

She glanced at Nick to see that he was watching her with a curious expression. She didn't know how she felt about his focus being on her so intently. Looking back at where Aiden stood a couple of dozen feet away by a sculpture of Santa and Mrs. Claus, she said, "I think I've pointed out doves enough around Christmastime that Aiden thinks they're practically magical. Well, he pretty much thinks all of Christmas is magical. It has always been one of my number one goals for him.

"A few years ago, I found some Christmas tree dove ornaments. They have real feathers on them with little clips where their feet are so they can clip on a branch. I got half a dozen of them. Aiden loves them so much! He always spends a lot of time at the tree each year, petting the doves with a single careful finger."

She glanced again at Nick, and this time, he was

looking at her with something different in his expression. A softness, for sure. But there was something else behind those eyes that she couldn't quite name that made her insides react in a way that she hadn't felt in a while. Was she so date-starved that a soft look would impact her so much? And why did she suddenly not know how to react?

She broke eye contact and said, "Wow. The kids haven't pulled us over to them even once. Should we be concerned?"

Nick nodded in their direction, where they were whispering something to each other, giggling. "Clearly, yes. That's the look of two kids plotting something."

The kids ran toward them, racing around a circle of miniature snowmen whose stick arms made it look like they were holding hands, and stopped right in front of her and Nick.

"Can we go on the train now?" Holly asked.

"Sure thing," Nick said.

Holly grabbed Nick's hand and Aiden grabbed Rachel's, and the two kids pulled them toward Santa's village and the kid-sized train that ran all around it. As they neared the arch where everyone lined up to ride on the train, Aiden stopped and said, "My hat is getting itchy," and took it off. "Will you wear it on your head?"

"I can hold it for you," she offered.

He shook his head. "No, it has to be over your hat."

Rachel looked over at Nick. It was clear by the look on his face that he hadn't heard the legend that said if you wear a Santa hat when you walk under the arch leading to the Christmas train that you'd fall in love. Based on the way Aiden and Holly were sharing looks and still giggling, Aiden had let Holly in on that little piece of knowledge. And Holly's dad was conveniently already wearing a Santa hat.

She took a deep breath. Of course, *she* didn't believe the myth, but Aiden did. Would wearing the hat give him false hope? Or would not wearing it take away a bit of the Christmas magic that he and Holly were feeling? It was obviously important to them.

She was suddenly picturing Courtney and Lucy standing there, reminding her that this was her Season of Yes and this choice counted.

It was not that big of a deal. She smiled at Aiden and said, "Okay, put it on me."

She crouched down and he struggled for a moment as he tried to fit the kid-sized Santa hat not only on an adult-sized head but on a head that was already wearing a knitted hat. Eventually, he just kind of balanced it there and she stood back up, trying to hold her head level so it wouldn't fall off. Both kids were so happy they were practically dancing. It was the right decision.

The giggling intensified as they walked under the arch. At least they were getting along.

There weren't too many people at the park right then, so it didn't take long before it was Aiden's and Holly's turn to get on the train. Nick had his phone out, ready to take pictures before Rachel even got a chance to pull out hers. They both took a few pictures, then Rachel just watched as Nick started videoing the train ride. She loved how attentive he was as a father. Between growing up with her dad, losing both of her parents, and then having Aiden at age twenty-four, she'd gathered quite the list of requirements for a future husband, and many of them had to do with how the guy might be as a dad.

Maybe that was why she dated so infrequently. It was hard to find someone who would be a great husband and a great dad, and who would be willing to step right into the dad role from day one. Why did she have to find someone who seemed perfect, but was still grieving his late wife?

Because it had been a very long time since she'd looked at a guy like she was now looking at Nick and felt such a strong attraction. The guy's nose, cheeks, and the tops of his ears were red from the cold, yet he was in Santa's village with his daughter, looking like he was loving every minute of it.

Courtney's words, "I think that's the sign of a guy with the capacity to love someone deeply" echoed in her head. That was what she was seeing—a man loving his daughter deeply.

The train was coming back around for its final time, and a few of the kids waiting to get on bumped into her in their excitement, pushing Rachel right into Nick. He wrapped his arms around her to steady her and keep her from knocking them both down.

"I got you," he said in a low tone. His voice, so close to her ear, her chest against his, his arms wrapped around her, sent warm shivers through her body. She stood frozen for a moment, so shocked at all the emotions coursing through her that she couldn't move.

"Mom!" Aiden shouted as he leaped off the train, not even looking over at her, his eyes glued to something by the gazebo that had wall panels to make it look like a gingerbread house. "I found a dove!"

Rachel mumbled "Thanks" to Nick, then straightened herself up to standing and not pressed into his embrace, her cheeks feeling not quite as cold as they were. She grabbed the Santa hat that had fallen from her head to his shoulder, then hurried to catch up to Aiden as he was making a beeline to the gazebo.

"I knew I'd find a dove here!" Aiden said as she caught up to him. The decoration was new—it was slightly bigger than an actual dove and was perched on a post right next to the gingerbread house. Aiden took off his gloves and reached down into his pocket to pull out a small, wrinkled, folded piece of paper.

"Is that your Christmas list?" Rachel asked him. "I thought you wanted to go give that to Santa."

Aiden shook his head as he worked the paper into the claw of the dove. "It's a Christmas *wish*."

She wasn't sure what the distinction was in his mind, but if she had to guess what was on it, it was a request for more paper. Her little crafty boy could never seem to get enough paper.

Nick and Holly caught up with them just as they turned and nearly bumped into Rachel's brother, Jack, as he came out of the gazebo with his fiancée, Noelle.

"Uncle Jack!" Aiden said, jumping up to give him a starfish hug before sliding back to the ground.

Rachel introduced her brother and Noelle to Nick and Holly. The entire time that Jack and Nick made small talk and shook hands, with Nick's focus entirely on Jack, Noelle's was on Rachel. She raised her eyebrows, grinning, and mouthed, "He's cute."

Rachel smiled, knowing that it wasn't just her who noticed. Of course, the more she got to know Nick, the cuter he became. Between today and working on the fireplace with him, the man had practically stepped up a good seventeen spaces on the attractiveness scale.

Noelle gave Rachel a questioning look that she knew meant "How serious are the two of you?" and Rachel loved that she instantly knew what Noelle was asking. For almost her entire life, she'd only had a brother. But after Saturday night, she'd finally have a sister. Well, technically a sister-in-law, but that was every bit as good. She couldn't think of a better gift her brother could give her.

Rachel gave a slight shrug, and Noelle seemed to understand that she wasn't quite sure what was going to happen between her and Nick and that it was much too early to try to pin a name to anything between them.

Aiden was talking to Holly, and Rachel finally tuned into what he was saying. "And there are so many things to put in the hot chocolate, and we get to go to the wedding on a hay ride and it's the best! It's so much fun and one of my favorite things about Christmas. And," Aiden said, puffing his chest out, "I even get to carry the rings at the wedding."

The more Aiden talked about how great everything was at an event that Holly wasn't invited to, the more Holly's expression became closed off and sour. She crossed her arms and looked at the ground, but also looked like she really would've just preferred kicking Aiden in the shins.

"Aiden," Rachel said, putting her hands on his shoulders and turning him toward the activities going on in the park, "maybe we should focus on everything here instead."

"Oh, hey," Noelle said, seeming to have a gift of

understanding what was going on between the kids, "you two should come to the wedding!"

Rachel shot her almost sister-in-law a look. She and Nick weren't even dating. This tonight wasn't even a date. Inviting him to a wedding where she and Aiden were the only people he would know meant that Noelle was basically setting the two of them up on a date. Asking while they were both present made it extra awkward to say no. But she was pretty sure Noelle didn't even feel bad about that.

No, it wasn't a date. Jack and Noelle were just inviting them to an event that was also going to be attended by a lot of family and friends.

"You should," Jack said. "We had a couple of people cancel because they are nervous about the weather, so we've got the space."

"No, we couldn't," Nick said. "This is your wedding, and you don't know us—"

"—Yet," Jack said.

Noelle nodded. "And that's why you should come. You're new in town, right? It'd be a good way to get to know people." She smiled at Holly. "And I bet Holly will love it."

Nick looked at Rachel like he was trying to see what she thought about it all. What was she even feeling? Nerves? Awkwardness? A thrill at having a reason to see him again in just three days? Anticipation? Excitement?

Worry that she was putting herself in a position to become even more attracted to a guy she shouldn't be attracted to? She was pretty sure she was feeling it all.

And, of course, she was right in the middle of her Season of Yes. That meant she *had* to say yes, right? She smiled at Nick. "Yes, you should come. It'll be fun."

Hopefully, it would turn out better than her purchase of the atrocious sweater they'd come across that Aiden thought she should buy because it "looked so cute."

eight

NICK

NICK STOOD in front of the closet doors that were made of mirrors in the guest room where he was staying at his in-laws' house. The mirrors were dated monstrosities that had startled him more than once when he walked past them at night when the lights were off, but they were sure helpful while he was getting ready.

His fingers kept fumbling as he was tying his tie, making him restart. What was he doing, going to the wedding of a couple he'd barely met, just because the groom's sister was the mom of one of the kids in his daughter's first grade class?

That wasn't why he was nervous, and he knew it. He was nervous because that mom was someone who made his heart beat faster every time he saw her. His breath catch. His chest floated like everything that had been weighing him down was suddenly lighter. As he was sitting at the desk in this cramped room, writing code or working through lines of code, trying to find exactly where an issue was, Rachel's smile started popping into his head. But not just every smile—the smiles she gave him, specifically. He was starting to crave those.

He glanced over to the wooden chair at the edge of the closet where Holly was sitting as she waited for him to get his suit coat and tie on. "Do I look okay?"

Holly stood up on her chair and motioned him over, so he walked up to her. She reached out and straightened his tie and then brushed her hands over his shoulders. "You look beautiful, Dad. Oh, wait. For boys, it's *handsome*, right? Rachel is going to see you and her eyes are going to bug out because you look so handsome."

He looked back at the mirror. Was that why he was so nervous? Was that what he wanted— for Rachel to see him and like what she saw? Yes, it was, he realized. So why did he feel so very not ready? Maybe because it had been so long since he'd been in the dating pool that he'd forgotten how to swim. He felt like he was in the shallow end, thinking someone really should put arm floaties on him before he waded out any further.

"Now this is the part where you tell me that I look like a beautiful princess."

He smiled at his daughter as she twisted from side to side on the chair, her poofy ankle-length dress swishing out as she did. "You look like a beautiful princess, Hollybear."

"Thanks!" she said and leaped off the chair. "Now let's get there already."

They said goodbye to Ben and Linda. Yes, they'd encouraged him to start dating, but it didn't make it feel any less weird to see them right before meeting someone who was not their daughter. It wouldn't be too much longer, though, before he would be finished with the renovations at the new house and he and Holly could move in.

They pulled up to the address that Rachel had given him, which was apparently the bride's parents' house. Strings of Christmas lights lined the house and lit up all the trees and shrubs. Santa's village and a manger scene decorated the lawn, and a couple of dozen people milled about all the decorations, kids chasing each other around everything. A truck with two flat-bed trailers loaded with bales of hay covered in blankets sat parked in front of the house.

Holly put her hands on her cheeks. "It's just so magical!"

They got out of the car, and Holly ran ahead, her golden dress bouncing below her blue winter coat, and Nick scanned the crowd for Rachel. He found her talking with a small group of people and started walking toward her. She was wearing a plum-colored dress coat and tall boots, the bottom of her dark green dress visible below the coat, and her dark hair pulled up all fancy. She looked stunning standing there in the middle of the snow and the Christmas decorations.

It took a moment before she glanced in his direction. The moment her eyes landed on him, her expression—the one that spontaneously appeared before she even would've had a chance to choose it—looked a lot like elated happiness. Something washed through him at seeing it. He wouldn't have been able to describe it, but it made his chest swell to know he evoked that reaction in her.

She was still smiling when he reached her and she said, "I'm so glad you two came. We are going to be loading up soon. Should we get some hot chocolate, first?"

Holly and Aiden both seemed to materialize at their side just then, almost like they knew the hot chocolate was coming. Rachel led them to a table filled with different hot chocolate mix-ins where Noelle's dad was pouring hot chocolate into cups with a ladle and handing them out.

As they were choosing their mix-ins, Holly asked, "Are these all the people that are coming to the wedding?"

Rachel glanced out at the crowd. "No—the hay ride can't fit everyone at once. This group is just us and

Noelle's parents, siblings, and their kids. Extended family will be arriving in a bit, and they'll ride over in the second group. Everyone else will just meet us at the chapel."

Holly's eyes grew as Rachel listed off who was coming, but all Nick could think was that they were in the wrong place. Everyone there was only close family. They were a last-minute addition, and it wasn't even a real date.

Not long after they got their hot chocolates, he heard a ringing and everyone's attention went to the bride and groom—Rachel's brother, Jack, and his soon-to-be wife, Noelle, whom they'd met three days ago. They stood at the top of the sloping yard, near the house. Jack was dressed in a fine-looking tux, and Noelle wore a white wedding dress with a white fur-lined coat that looked kind of like a cape and went all the way to the ground. They were both grinning and holding champagne glasses filled with hot chocolate.

"We want to thank you all for coming," Jack said. "It means a lot to us."

Noelle smiled. "This is not the most traditional start to a wedding, we know, but we wanted to celebrate with you in a way that we most love celebrating."

Jack said, "Noelle was my employee a year ago when we last had this hot chocolate and hay ride activity, and I had some pretty high walls up. It was sitting on that second trailer right over there when I first let those walls come down for a minute. It felt appropriate to have this lead to our wedding."

"Cheers!" Noelle said, holding her hot chocolate up high.

Everyone else held theirs up and shouted "Cheers!" right back.

They all took their hot chocolates with them and climbed onto the trailers, the bride and groom sitting on hay bales stacked two high on the first trailer, facing everyone.

Aiden initially sat down next to Rachel, but in true six-year-old fashion, only stayed there for about five seconds before he jumped up to sit next to the woman Nick had figured out was Noelle's mom. So Nick took the opportunity to sit right next to Rachel. The story Jack told about this hay ride was pretty sweet. It surprised him that he was suddenly wanting the same thing to happen to him.

Someone started Christmas music playing, and Rachel motioned to a woman who was videoing everything with her phone and leaned in close to him to say, "That's Noelle's sister, Katie. She interviews the family at the Christmas activities and makes a video to show on Christmas Eve."

She continued, telling him who all the people were on both trailers, but there were so many names and he was so distracted by her nearness. The peppermint scent of her hair. The feel of her warm breath against his cheek.

Holly had been right when they pulled up. There was a sort of magic here.

His attention, right along with Rachel's, went to Aiden as the boy said to Noelle's mom, "So what do I call you after Uncle Jack gets married?"

Mrs. Allred cocked her head. "Call me?"

"I'll get to start calling Noelle 'Aunt Noelle,' but I don't know what I'm supposed to call you."

"Well, technically, we still won't be related."

Aiden frowned, his eyebrows pulling together. "No, we have to be related. Won't you be my grandma-in-law or something?"

The woman chuckled as she put an arm around Aiden and pulled him into her side. Then she told him a story about how where she grew up, they referred to found or adopted family as hanai and said that they were hanai now. "So, as hanai, what would you like to call me?"

Aiden pointed at the boy on her other side, who looked about his age. "Tommy calls you Grandma. Can I call you that, too?"

"You sure can."

Nick stole a glance at Rachel and saw the most elated smile on her face. It must've meant a lot to her that this family that was soon to be her brother's was also claiming them.

On Nick's other side, Holly tugged on his coat sleeve, then she got to her knees so she could whisper in his ear, trying to surreptitiously point to Noelle's mom. "If you and Rachel get married, will I be able to call her Grandma, too?"

The question caught him off guard so much that he was almost too stunned to answer. He hadn't thought Holly would've connected so many dots with him and Rachel, and he wasn't sure if he should be worried that she was starting to form connections with her friend's uncles in-law.

"Um, I don't know, honey. I guess we should wait and see." It wasn't the best answer, and he knew it. But he hadn't prepared himself for questions like that.

"WOULD YOU LIKE TO DANCE?" Nick asked, holding a hand out to Rachel, who was seated at a table.

He soaked in the smile she gave him as she set down her drink and stood, putting her hand in his. When they reached a good spot on the dance floor, he put one arm around Rachel's waist and held her hand with his other, just like his mom had taught him and his siblings all those years ago at the army base in Fort Leavenworth, Kansas.

As they moved to the music, so in sync, he reveled in the feel of her in his arms and felt himself fall for her just a bit more, like he had been all night.

Shortly after they'd arrived, he and Holly went with Aiden and Rachel, where Rachel and Katie were prepping Aiden to be the ring bearer. As they told Aiden about how special and important his role was and what exactly he needed to do, Nick could see Holly getting surlier and surlier.

He understood that Holly felt bad that Aiden was getting so much attention and was being assigned a cool job and Holly wasn't. But the groom was someone very important in Aiden's life and Holly had just barely met the guy.

Holly getting upset and jealous seemed to happen a lot lately, which told Nick that she was struggling to adjust to the big move. And since she didn't know anyone well except for Aiden, she was kind of taking it all out on him. He was about to crouch down to Holly's height and talk to her about it. What he'd say, exactly, he wasn't sure. It wasn't like anything he could say would make her less jealous in the moment.

But before he could, Rachel turned to Holly. "And I have a huge and important job I could use your help with."

Holly perked right up, all signs of dejection falling from her demeanor. "You do?'

Rachel nodded and took her by the hand to a small table by the doors that led into the chapel. It held the guest book and a basket of something. She told Holly that they wanted all the guests to toss rose petals as the couple came back down the aisle after getting married and that each guest needed a pouch of roses. They'd be coming soon, and she wanted her to hand one to each guest.

He was sure that the plan had been to just leave the basket on the table for each guest to pick up their own, but by the time Rachel finished talking with Holly, Holly was convinced that her job was the most important one of the entire wedding. He'd watched Rachel as she'd pulled off the magic, feeling his chest warming, his heart being tugged, that she would care so much for his daughter. What she had done had completely changed how the evening was likely to go, and he was so grateful to her for it.

But his feelings hadn't stopped at gratitude. He'd fallen some more. The kind that left his stomach whooshing.

He'd sat next to her during the wedding ceremony and watched as she'd beamed at her son, walking up the aisle in his little suit, acting so proper yet with a wide grin on his face, and he'd had the thought *When Clara said she wanted me to get remarried, this was the kind of person she was imagining.* And he fell for Rachel a bit more.

It was just Jack and Noelle and the officiant at the front of the room, which felt so perfect for the venue and the crowd. They'd both written their own vows, which made practically the entire chapel start reaching for the tissues. When Rachel's brother said, "I had always hated Christmas and thought it was impossible to get past it," Rachel grabbed Nick's hand. He gave it a squeeze as Rachel sniffed, dabbing at her tears with a tissue in her other hand.

"You came along and changed everything," Jack had said. "I spent most of my life figuring that I would never find 'the one.' Then you walked into my office for an interview and I knew that day that you were it. But I spent the next year and a half thinking that a relationship with you was impossible." He'd smiled at Noelle. "I should've known that, once again, you'd find a way to make the impossible possible.

"I've seen it time and time again since then, and I can't wait to spend the rest of my life with you, knowing that nothing is impossible."

He'd gotten choked up hearing Jack's vows, too. Between the words, the way they were said, and the looks that Jack and Noelle had given each other, it was impossible not to.

"I wish my parents were here," Rachel had said, her words barely a whisper. He looked over at her, studying her. She hadn't talked much about them, but so many emotions filled her face. And then she'd leaned into him, putting her head on his shoulder. So he put his arm around her shoulders and he felt himself fall further.

All during the refreshments and chatting with guests, whenever his eyes weren't on Holly, they were on Rachel. Everything about her, from the way her eyes crinkled when she smiled, to how freely she laughed, to how she always seemed to have all the details of everything in her head and knew just when to check on something or get something, to how she made everyone around her feel made him feel like he was falling. Hopelessly falling.

And now that they were dancing together and all the emotions he'd been experiencing all night felt like they were wrapped in the bubble of the two of them dancing, he didn't just feel like he was falling. He felt like he'd been pushed out of an airplane. The parachute hadn't been deployed—he was just free-falling and taking in the landscape and the exhilarating feel of the wind rushing past his face.

A part of his heart had been so damaged when Clara died. But even though he'd known it had been damaged, he'd ignored it and pushed on because being a single dad was hard. Being a single dad who was grieving was even harder. Some things, like that pain in his heart, he'd just learned to live with. It had become his new normal.

But tonight, he'd felt things starting to shift and heal and not hurt so much. Just being around Rachel brought a lightness that he hadn't felt in a very long time.

He swung her out and she laughed as she twirled back into him, ending with her back against his front, and he held her for a moment as they swayed to the music. He'd seen her laughing so much tonight. That had done something to his heart, too, especially when he was the one who had made her laugh. Feeling her close to him, her breath tickling his neck did something else to his heart and made him feel things he hadn't for so long.

As they moved around the dance floor to a faster-paced song, they saw Holly making up crazy dances with Aiden and Noelle's nieces and nephews. Holly looked so happy. Maybe her heart was healing, too.

"There's so much I still don't know about you," Nick said. "And I find myself wanting to know everything."

Rachel smiled. "Me, too. What's your favorite topping on a pizza? I mean, it's not the deepest question ever, but if we're ever going to share a pizza, it's vital information to know ahead of time."

So she was thinking about the future and seeing him in it. He was smiling with his whole face when he said,

"Can it even be called a pizza if there isn't pepperoni on it? But my favorite beyond that is black olives."

"Olives? Interesting. Mine is chicken."

"Chicken? I don't understand. Like, along with the pepperoni?"

Her arms were still around his neck, but she lifted her shoulders in a slight shrug. "With or without. I like it all ways."

"Huh. Okay. If you had to play an Olympic sport, what would it be?"

She bit her lip as she thought. "Hmm. I'm going to have to go with the bobsled. I'm not the most athletic person, and for that one, it's mostly about the leaning, right? You?"

He laughed. "Um, ski jumping, maybe?" He hadn't ever done it before, but it probably felt a lot like what his stomach was experiencing now. Was he feeling all these emotions just because they were at a wedding? He'd been a sap for weddings ever since he'd had his own. Maybe what he was feeling was just because of the situation and their surroundings. It felt like more than that, though, and he had to know for sure. "Let's go on a date."

Rachel's eyebrows rose. He was hoping in interest.

"Not because we have a project or because something else pulled us together. Let's go because we want to. Just the two of us."

Rachel bit her lip as she glanced over his shoulder at where their kids were dancing, and it was killing him to not know what was going through her mind right then. Then her eyes met his again. "I would like that."

He held back the smile that threatened to overtake his face and forced himself to play it cool as they moved to the music. "I would love to take you out on a Friday or a Saturday, but I don't want to wait that long to see you again. How does Tuesday sound?" He had *just* told himself to play it cool and then he says something like that? He was so out of practice. But also, he really did want to see her.

She bit her lip and once again, he wished he could hear her thoughts. "I'll have to see if I can find a sitter for that soon. Bria has finals this week. I would ask Jack and Noelle, but the house they bought isn't ready for them yet, so they're staying in Golden, and that's probably a bit far."

"My in-laws are always free on Tuesdays. Would you like me to ask if they'd mind watching Aiden, too?"

She glanced over at where Aiden was doing a dance that looked a little like T-Rex trying not to step on Legos and failing miserably. Holly and the other two boys were trying to mimic him but were unable to because they were holding their stomachs from laughing so hard.

"I'd really like that."

After they got home that night and after he got Holly

in bed, he walked into his temporary bedroom, feeling like he was still on a high from the entire evening. He loosened his tie, unbuttoned the top button, and flopped down on his bed, opening his phone.

He swiped to the last screen and smiled at Clara's picture. "I met someone and I really like her. Her name is Rachel. I know—it feels weird to come to you to talk about this, but you were my best friend and the first person I always told everything to. You told me that you wanted me to start dating again, so here I am, dating again.

"I think you'd like her, too. She's a great mom and she is so good with Holly. If you've been keeping an eye on us, I'm sure you already know that. But I wanted to tell you that you were right—I've felt so alone since you died, but tonight, I experienced how great it feels to not be so alone. So thank you."

He turned off the phone and marveled at how excited he could be for a Tuesday.

nine

RACHEL

RACHEL LEANED in close to the mirror as she applied mascara. Aiden sat on the side of the bathtub, swinging his legs so that his heels hit the bathtub, making a reverberating thudding sound. He'd already asked questions about what she and Nick were going to be doing, what she thought he and Holly were going to do with Holly's grandparents, and if he got to stay up late.

Those questions she fielded like a pro. She'd also fielded texts from Courtney and Lucy about the date and what things she'd said yes to today like a pro. But when Aiden asked, "Is Nick going to be my dad?" she jerked enough that she swiped the mascara wand across the skin beside her eye.

After Aiden was born, she always thought that when she got serious with someone, she would have time to figure out how much she liked them and would only introduce them to Aiden once she was sure about the relationship. She didn't want him forming his own opinions before she got a chance to form her own, and she definitely didn't want him getting attached if things weren't going to work out.

But since it was through Aiden that she met Nick, that plan went out the window. Nothing about this was going as planned. What she needed to do was set some expectations and be as honest as she could with him.

She grabbed a tissue, got it a little wet, and then started wiping the mascara off. "I don't know, buddy, because I don't know how much we like each other yet. We probably won't know until we've been on a few more dates—it hasn't been nearly long enough for us to start thinking about things like that." Not that the thought hadn't crossed her mind more than a time or two or a thousand. Honestly, though, she was surprised that Aiden had gotten there already.

"But you like him," Aiden said, dragging out the word "like" as he did a little torso dance while still sitting. Then he stood to add more extravagance to his dance. "You really like him."

Her cheeks suddenly went pinker than the blush

she'd already put on as she thought about how much she did like Nick. Everything had changed Saturday night at the wedding. There had been so many moments when he'd just been thoughtful or a sweet father or had looked at her with an expression of adoration that made her knees weak. So many things he'd said all night long had made her fall just a little bit more for him.

And there had definitely been moments when a fire built in her chest that made her want to grab him by the front of his suit jacket and pull him to her so he could kiss her senseless.

They'd texted back and forth on Sunday so much and he'd been so charming and witty and fun. She couldn't wait until Tuesday to see him and eventually invited him and Holly over that night. She and Aiden had planned to do their annual snowflake creating tradition—which he'd gotten a jump start on weeks ago—and get them hung from the ceiling. Aiden was thrilled that more people would be joining in on a tradition that was one of his favorites.

She'd known that she'd love having Nick and his daughter join them. What she hadn't anticipated was watching Nick's shoulder and arm muscles flex as he climbed onto the step ladder to tape each of the snowflake's strings to their ceiling. That had brought its own joy to her world.

"I do like him. How about you?"

Aiden shrugged, looking so nonchalant, even though he hadn't managed to wipe the smile completely off his face. "He's cool."

RACHEL WALKED hand-in-hand with Nick down Main Street, both of them sipping from cups of warm wassail, looking at all the lights and decorations just as snow started to softly fall. Everything about the evening had been perfect. The dinner, the conversation, and now that they were just out enjoying the season, the feeling that there wasn't anywhere else they needed to be, the peace.

"This feels straight out of *It's a Wonderful Life*," she said.

"Except in color."

"And I'm not wearing a dress."

"That's downright scandalous." Nick pulled his phone out of his pocket. "What do you say to a selfie to remember the occasion?"

She snuggled in close to him as they both smiled at the phone camera. She had to admit that they looked pretty cute next to each other.

"You know, Jimmy is my middle name."

She looked over at Nick. "Really. Your full name is Nicholas Jimmy Stewart?"

He laughed. "No, my middle name is Buckles."

"Buckles?"

"Hey, don't knock it. It was my maternal grandpa's last name." He paused a moment. "And his first name was Jimmy."

She gave him a playful smack on the arm. "It was not."

"True story. We went to Grandpa Jimmy and Grandma Ina's farm every year growing up."

As he told about it, the feeling of peace with him settled in more deeply. She had not been expecting that emotion at all. Lately, with all she had been saying yes to, she'd been feeling rather overwhelmed. She was trying to do all the traditions that she and Aiden had developed over the years, like the snowflakes and their Christmas movie marathon. Then all the town events, like the Christmas sing-in they went to last night. And then after last year, they'd added several traditions with Noelle's big family, and every night she was coming home from work and hurrying to get Aiden ready for the next thing.

And all the Christmas shopping. She couldn't forget that.

New relationships took time, too. Time she was more

than happy to spend. Each time her phone dinged with a new text from Nick, her heart lit up like the big tree in Downtown Park.

As busy as the Season of Yes was making her, saying yes to a date with Nick was calming her stressed heart in ways she hadn't even guessed it would do.

But still, whenever she was with him, thoughts of his late wife would inevitably pop into her head. It was clear that he loved her. That he still did. Which was honestly super endearing. She was glad that he did and that he kept Clara alive in Holly's thoughts. She wouldn't want anything different from him. She just didn't know how that would affect how he felt about *her.*

"Do you mind if I ask how Clara died?" She probably should've eased her way into the question. But she'd wanted to ask for a while, and it felt like it needed to be soon. Probably not blurting-it-out soon, but it was too late to pull it back.

He didn't seem taken aback that she asked—he just looked up at the falling snow, one of the flakes landing on an eyelash before speaking. "From a heart condition she'd probably had since she was young that none of us knew about. We were completely blindsided. I only knew there was a problem when she didn't show up to the school to pick up Holly from kindergarten as she had planned."

"Oh. That must have been so hard."

"It really was."

She had an overwhelming urge to just hold him close and make everything better, but she didn't know what to say. Instead of saying something comforting, she heard the words, "I had cancer" come from her mouth.

Nick's steps halted momentarily.

"Last year," she continued, "Acute Myeloid Leukemia. It was rough, but even with as rough as it got, I never worried that I wouldn't be there for Aiden as he grew up. I always had a gut feeling that I would make it through to the very end. And I did—my scan six months ago came back clean."

She could tell he was rattled, but she didn't know what to do about that. The cancer was simply a fact. One that she worried could very well scare him away, especially after losing his wife.

"Everything is good now, then?" His voice wavered a bit, but she could tell he was trying to make the words come out strong and confident.

She shrugged. "I mean, yeah. Everything looks good so far. It was an aggressive cancer, but I had age and a good health history on my side. A lot of things really went my way, actually."

"That must have been intense. I'm very glad to hear you made it through." They walked in silence for several long moments. She stayed quiet, knowing that he needed time to process.

He must not have wanted to process out loud, though, because he changed the subject. "Do you mind if I ask about Aiden's dad?"

Rachel wondered if the question had been as burning to him as asking about his wife had been for her. It took a moment to think about how to even explain because there was so much more to it than the short version.

"That's not something I can explain in a sentence or two."

Nick gestured at all the lights and decorations on Main Street and at the soft snow that felt like it was almost glowing from the light strands crossing over Main Street. "I can walk up and down this street with you as many times as needed. Ten? A hundred? You've got it."

She chuckled and secretly swooned. How long had it been since she'd been on a date when the guy was so interested in everything she said? Long enough ago that she couldn't remember.

"Okay, then. Um, to explain, I need to go back to age eighteen when my parents died. Jack was fifteen, and the night they got in that wreck was the night I first became a parent."

That had been a dozen years ago, yet it was still hard to bring up. Probably because bringing it up always brought back the emotions she'd felt that night when the officer knocked on their door. So much had changed at that moment. More than she could comprehend. All she'd felt was the whirlwind in her mind, the stabbing pain in her gut, the ache in her heart. It took days, weeks, and months to begin to understand all the emotions that came with the news.

"But at least I'd had a lot of practice with parenting before then—our mom struggled with a lot of things and would often check out for weeks at a time. But it was different once it was only the two of us. Jack started acting out and kind of lost his way a bit."

"That's a completely understandable reaction. Losing both parents at the same time had to be tough."

She nodded, feeling the truth of that statement deep in her bones. She had been dealing with her own grief all while trying to be everything Jack needed her to be. And that was on top of simply being eighteen and trying to figure out how to be an adult and make the decisions that would impact her future so much.

"Jack didn't go to college right after high school. I think all of those first years were hard, but that one was especially tough for a lot of reasons. But then he figured out what he wanted to do and what he needed to do to get there and started college just a year late. He lived with me that year—we were both in college. That was a great year.

"Then I graduated and he moved into a dorm on

campus with some friends, and a friend moved into my place as my roommate. I just felt...” She wasn't even sure how to express what the emotions had been like that year. “Adrift, maybe? I think I had gotten so used to being the parent, the one in charge, and I didn't know how to *not* have Jack to look after. It had become a good part of my identity, I think.

“I mean, don't get me wrong— it was great to not have so much responsibility piled on me. But I suddenly no longer had school to focus on and I was working a job I hated that had nothing to do with my degree and Jack was doing great and didn't need me so much.

“After having to be the responsible one since I was young, I kind of had my own rebellious moment and made some less-than-great choices. At the same time, though, I felt a bit like...” She paused. “I don't know, like an empty nester, maybe? I think I was just really craving someone in my life to take care of. And those two things didn't mix well.

“So I dated a crappy guy. And one night, the crappy telephone customer service job I had laid everyone off the same day that my roommate announced that she was moving out of state. I was feeling extra rebellious and in need of someone. It was one night of poor decisions, and before long, I found out I was pregnant.”

She glanced at Nick, almost afraid to see his reaction, but the look on his face was that of concern. Undivided attention. And something else. Understanding without judgment, maybe? Whatever it was, it made her whole chest feel warm and light even as the snow fell all around them.

"Anyway, I let the guy know, and he was mad because it didn't fit with his life plans. The day I told him was the last time I ever saw him. Eventually, a lawyer delivered papers where he'd signed away his parental rights and asked me never to contact him again. He didn't even know when Aiden was born because he never wanted to."

She looked at Nick again, and he was breathing heavily, eyebrows drawn together like he was ready to stand up to the guy right then and let him know what he thought of it all and her breath caught. She hadn't experienced a guy outside of her brother who had ever shown that kind of protectiveness of her before. He shook his head. "I can't even fathom not wanting to be there—to even know—your own kid."

She studied his expression, drinking in the look on his face that came with that statement. It was so authentic and it pulled at her heart.

"It might have been a decision I regretted making, and I definitely wouldn't have chosen the timing." She shook her head. "Those first few years were *so* hard. But in the end, I got Aiden. And he means the world to me."

"And he's a great kid," Nick said.

They stopped, right there at the winter wonderland display in front of Trove of Oldies and she just nodded as she looked into Nick's eyes. His hat and the shoulders of his coat were covered in snow—she hadn't noticed that it had started coming down so much—and the air was cold enough that each of their breaths were little puffs of clouds.

But those eyes of his were warm. Inviting. Full of all the things she'd been hoping for, both consciously and subconsciously, since the day she'd found out she was going to have a baby.

And he was looking at her like he really saw her. All of her. He wasn't ignoring any parts of her that he didn't like—he was looking at her like she didn't even have parts that he didn't like. Like she was everything just the way she was, and she'd never felt so accepted.

His eyes flicked to her lips, and suddenly she couldn't think of anything she wanted more than to have his lips on hers. She took a step toward him, and the look of longing on his face intensified. A snowflake fell right on his cheek and melted. He closed the gap between them, and suddenly the snow and the cold felt just beyond them. There was nothing between them but warmth and peace.

He reached with two fingers to brush the snow-covered hair away from her cheek, and the touch of his fingers sent a tingling warmth through her whole body.

Then she heard a buzzing sound and he looked at his watch, his eyebrows pulling together. "Oh. It's my mother-in-law." He pulled his phone from his pocket and answered it, putting it on speakerphone. "Hello?" His voice was concerned.

"I'm so sorry to bother you on your date." Rachel recognized Linda's voice from when she'd met her just before their date.

"Are Holly and Aiden okay?"

"Now don't panic."

"Linda, that's not helping me not to panic. Are they okay?"

"They were just playing in the snow and Holly jumped off the porch and landed on one of those big rocks in the flower beds—she didn't see it because of the snow—and hurt her ankle. Ben says it's not broken and it's not bad enough to need a doctor, but it still hurts. She just—"

"We'll be right there." He said goodbye and looked at Rachel. "I'm so sorry to end things early. That is not what I would have chosen."

She smiled at him, loving that he would be willing to end things early to look out for his daughter. Out of every moment tonight, that might have made her fall for him the most.

And it was also the most quintessentially parental thing that possibly could've happened tonight. So much so, that she should have known without a doubt that it would happen. But boy did she wish that the kiss that had seemed so inevitable moments ago had happened. She could almost feel how sweet his lips would be against hers.

ten

NICK

"DADDY, MY ANKLE HURTS," Holly said as they
sat on a blanket on the floor of what would very soon be
their dining area, having dinner with Rachel and Aiden.

"Maybe this will help," Rachel said as she took off
her cardigan, rolled it up, and then placed it under
Holly's ankle.

Holly looked up at Rachel like... well, like she'd
found something that was lost. He understood the
feeling so well.

Holly's ankle hadn't been injured too badly, but he
did keep her home from school on Wednesday. Luckily,
it hadn't been a day where he'd had to go into the office.
His office in his in-laws' home was in the guest bedroom
with him, so he had set up a bunch of pillows in his bed
like a throne. Holly had felt like a princess as she

colored, read, and watched shows on his tablet, Rosy by her side as he worked.

She seemed to have loved the extra attention and privileges... to a point. By that evening, she was tired of being in bed and wanted to play with Rosy. Linda had fixed her up with a simple ankle wrap, and despite a small limp, she seemed to play without any pain.

He'd taken her with him to the house every evening, and when she wasn't thinking about it, her ankle seemed to be pretty fine. He suspected that it was the attention that Rachel was giving her that was making it "hurt" tonight.

Even with Holly's ankle, he'd managed to finish the rest of the flooring and baseboard and trim Wednesday night and painted them just yesterday. He and Rachel had tentatively planned to finish the fireplace set piece on Saturday, but since the house was now ready to be moved into, he'd asked her if she could come tonight, instead.

Tomorrow, he and Holly were going to be able to move in. A full week before Christmas. He couldn't believe he'd managed to pull it all off.

As soon as they were done with the meal and got everything packed back up in the basket Rachel had brought, they let the dogs back through the gate. One of the only items in the house that wasn't a home improvement tool was a Bluetooth speaker he'd brought so he could listen to music while he worked on the house. He started it playing Christmas music and turned on the fireplace—it seemed appropriate, given what they'd be working on.

Then he and Rachel started working on the set piece. They hadn't even gotten through talking about their next steps before Aiden said, "Can me and Holly go set up the blankets for our beds?"

It would take hours to get the set piece finished and they knew they would be working past the kids' bedtimes, so they brought a huge pile of blankets and a couple of soft mats that his in-laws had so they could sleep when it was time. "Sure thing. Holly can show you which room."

The kids carried armloads of blankets away, trying not to trip on the trailing end, the dogs running around them and nipping at the corners of the blankets. He guessed there was going to be a lot of chaos and laughing and probably the wearing of blankets like capes before any beds got made. He was going to drink in every second of laughter that he heard coming from his daughter.

He and Rachel looked at the fireplace—the fake one, not the real one— which was standing but was still wood-colored. "So," Rachel said, her hand on her hips as she studied the piece, "paint from the mantle up first, so it can dry, then work on cutting and installing the brick facade? Then, hopefully, the top will be dry enough that we can paint the details and then figure out how to attach the Christmas decorations."

"Sounds like a good plan to me." He still had the floors covered with a drop cloth from when he'd painted this room yesterday, so they were able to get to work quickly. As Rachel painted the edges with the paintbrush and he painted the big areas with the roller, every time they got close to one another, he was reminded of their date on Tuesday and how they'd been moments away from kissing before it had abruptly ended. All the nerve endings firing, all the warmth spreading from his chest, all the longing that he'd been feeling that night he was feeling at full force again now.

And every time that their faces were close and Rachel's eyes would meet his, a breath of anticipation hanging in the air between them, a kid would come running into the room, usually chased by a dog, sometimes chasing a dog, and he'd be reminded how much a kiss wasn't about to happen. Holly was warming up to Rachel quite a bit, but if his daughter caught him and Rachel kissing, he worried it would be pushing her too far, much too fast.

Besides, every time he thought again about the kiss they'd almost shared, he would also start thinking again about the cancer. He knew cancer well enough to know that relapses could happen and that Rachel wouldn't fully be in the clear until she'd had scans come back clean for a full five years.

When she'd first told him, it had felt like a bowling ball hit him in the gut. He was really falling for Rachel. After losing Clara, though, could he face the possibility of losing Rachel, too? He wasn't sure.

They had gotten all the fake brick pieces cut that they would need and were in the middle of attaching them to the fireplace with the construction adhesive when Holly and Aiden came running into the room. "Can we each have one of those cookies you bought?" Holly asked.

"Yep," he said. "Just make sure the dogs don't eat any."

Somewhere in the middle of his sentence, he heard Rachel say "Oh," as an exhale.

"I apologize," he said. "I shouldn't have answered for both of us."

"No, it's totally fine. Go ahead, kids."

She might have said it was fine, but he'd seen from that initial look on her face that she wouldn't have told them it was okay. He glanced at the clock and realized that it was almost bedtime. Maybe saying yes to sugar wasn't the best idea ever.

"Yes!" Aiden pumped his fist. Then, to Holly, he said, "I told you she would say yes to anything!" Then the two of them ran over to the kitchen counter to get the cookies before racing off, the dogs at their heels.

He wouldn't have thought anything of Aiden's statement if it weren't for the way it made Rachel's cheeks redden, so he had to ask. "You'd say yes to anything?"

Her cheeks went redder and she rubbed her nose and then waved her hand. "It's just a bet with my coworkers. I'm doing a 'Season of Yes' because they think I'm too much of a planner and it'd be good for me."

Oh, interesting. He'd seen glimpses of her planning side, like when he'd seen inside her perfectly organized pantry when he and Holly had joined them for snowflake making, and anytime she opened her planner or the schedule in her phone, and when she'd unzipped her purse to grab lip balm, but he suddenly wondered how many things she'd said yes to that she wouldn't have chosen to do. "So, saying yes to helping with this set piece. Was it because of the bet?"

"I *definitely* only said yes because of the bet. I didn't have the first clue how to make this on my own."

"Going on a date with me?"

"Yes, because of the bet."

Oh.

She gave him a playful shove. "I'm kidding. That I *couldn't* have said no to."

The tension he hadn't realized had gathered in his shoulders released and a smile spread across his face.

Rachel grabbed the caulking gun with the adhesive, knelt in front of the fake fireplace, and started spreading the glue where the next faux brick section would go. Since the answer to the last question was, apparently, good for his shoulder muscles, he thought it might be fun to push it some more.

"And what about saying yes to coming over tonight? Was that because of the bet?"

She tapped a finger on her lips like she was deep in thought, and all he could think of was kissing those lips. "Well, I might not have changed plans... I was really looking forward to the wrapping presents party Aiden and I were going to have. But it turns out that going three days without seeing you is about my max."

Nick grabbed the next piece of bricks they had cut, knelt in front of the fireplace, and he and Rachel both fit it into the correct spot, both pressing on it for the thirty seconds the adhesive called for. Their shoulders were touching, their arms entangled, their knees bumping. "So what would've happened if we didn't work on this until tomorrow as we'd originally planned?"

Rachel shrugged. "I might have, say, gotten stuck in the wreaths at The Home Improvement Store and had to call for help. It's hard to say."

He shook his head, chuckling.

Aiden popped up from behind the kitchen island and

said, "Mom said that we would probably make gingerbread cookies and bring some to you!"

Rachel put a hand over her face. "Aiden! What are you doing spilling all my secrets?" Then she looked down at her watch. "Oh, wow. I didn't realize it was that late. It's bedtime."

The kids got their teeth brushed and pajamas on, then he and Rachel worked together to get the kids and the dogs all snuggled into their makeshift beds. Aiden pulled out the Christmas book that he had packed and Rachel read it to them.

After the book, as they were both straightening the blankets on their kids, Aiden said to Rachel, "You know that paper I left for the dove in the park? I want to tell you what I wished for but I can't say it out loud or it won't come true." He paused a moment, then said, "So how about I whisper it in your ear?"

Competitive girl that she was, Holly had to whisper something in Nick's ear while Aiden was whispering in his mom's. She motioned for him to come close, then cupped her hands between her mouth and his ear and said, "I think I am ready for a mom."

He pulled back, blown away by Holly's declaration. She was? He just looked at her for a moment as she gave a satisfied smile and lay back on her pillow again. Then she and Aiden shared a look, probably because she also whispered something into a parent's ear. He took

Rachel's lead and said goodnight to the kids before quietly leaving the room.

The whole evening—having dinner, working on a project together while the kids and the dogs played, tucking the kids in bed, all of it—had just felt so... domestic. Which was especially incredible, considering that they were in an empty house that hadn't been moved into. Regardless, it had almost felt like they were a family and it stirred something in him that made him crave more of it.

It took hours after the kids were asleep to finish all the details on the fireplace and get it fully decked out for Christmas, complete with stockings hanging on the mantle. But he didn't mind even a little bit, because it meant he got to spend more time with Rachel.

They swapped stories about their lives. He told her about his two sisters and brother and all the places they'd lived when he was growing up, and she told him funny stories about her and Jack and all the crazy things they'd done as kids. There were times when they'd laughed so hard that he was surprised they didn't wake Holly and Aiden.

He glanced at his watch—just past midnight. They took a seat on the hearth of his actual fireplace and admired the work they'd done on the fake one. "I kind of wish this was staying in my house—it makes the place feel more homey and Christmassy."

He caught a slight smile from Rachel out of the corner of his eye. "Of course, you moving in tomorrow will probably do the same thing."

He laughed. "True."

They gazed at it in silence for a moment before Rachel said, "We make a good team."

"We do." His voice came out lower, huskier than he'd meant. But the words were authentic—they'd made a great team. He stopped looking at their project so he could turn his gaze to her. They'd been working hard for many hours, but she still looked beautiful. Vibrant. Full of life. Her eyes still radiated spunk and caring kindness. She'd pulled her hair up into a ponytail when they'd started working, and it exposed the most exquisite neck.

All night long and really, since their date on Tuesday, they'd had so many little touches. A brushing of their hands or arms. A bumping of their shoulders or legs. And so many times when it happened, Rachel had given him a look that started a fire in his chest. And he could tell by how often she glanced at his lips that she was wanting a kiss as badly as he was.

But between the presence of the kids and the fact that the project had to be finished tonight—the rest of the weekend would be filled with moving in and the program was on Monday—the anticipation had been building and building.

But right now, she was there with him. No kids

present, no project looming over them. Christmas music played softly from the speaker across the room, the warmth from the fire was at their backs, the sounds of fire crackling just behind them.

Rachel reached out and ran a finger lightly across his forearm and the touch sent tingles up his arm. He met her eyes, his heart racing. Not because of anything to do with Clara. Or because he felt like he shouldn't kiss Rachel—it was more because he felt like he *should*. He hadn't expected that at all.

He just studied Rachel's face and took in everything that she was. The person she was. Everything about this moment just felt right.

Like they had all night long, their legs bumped together as he leaned in closer to her and she closed the gap, pressing her lips against his. Her lips were soft and the feel of them on his made him moan. Rachel sank into the kiss, a humming sigh escaping her that made that heat in his chest burn stronger.

He stood, pulling Rachel to stand with him, and put his hands on the sides of her face, savoring the feel of her skin, the touch of her lips, the scent of her shampoo, the tickle of her breath.

He dropped a hand to her waist to cradle her close to him, and she slid her hands up to his neck, sending tingles everywhere her fingertips touched.

When they'd been dancing at the wedding, he'd felt

like he'd been pushed out of an airplane, feeling the wind brush past his face. He had that same sense now, but this time, it was as if Rachel was falling with him, hand-in-hand, and he didn't care that the parachute hadn't deployed yet. The feeling of falling so completely and totally was consuming.

He pulled away from her lips so he could trail kisses along her jaw and down that neck that had looked so striking all night. Then he trailed the kisses right back up toward her ear and breathed, "You are an incredible woman."

The sound that escaped her lips may have been a moan. Or maybe a sigh. Whatever it was, it sounded both relaxed and elated and made his chest expand. She looked into his eyes, and he realized that he could stare into her eyes for hours and not tire of what he saw.

"Wow," she whispered. "That was..." She didn't finish her sentence and she didn't need to. She just looked into his eyes for a long moment, both of them soaking in everything.

Then her gaze shifted to behind him. She squinted, her eyebrows drawing together. "When did it start to snow?"

Still with his arm around her waist, he twisted to see the window that faced his backyard. The light inside made it reflect the surroundings of the room, but he could kind of see a bit of what lay beyond the window.

Rachel grabbed his hand and pulled him toward the doors that led onto his patio, so he turned the knob and pulled it open.

Snow had blanketed everything and was still falling gently, silently from the sky in big fat snowflakes. If this house contained anything other than a fake fireplace, a bunch of tools, and the blankets that their kids used, he might have welcomed the sight. He might have even suggested that he and Rachel go out on the patio, wrapped in blankets, and enjoy the storm together.

But neither of them was staying there tonight, so the falling snow brought with it a sense of urgency. He turned and hurried across the room and down the hall toward the front door and opened it. White covered everything, shining brightly in the light of the street lamps and Christmas lights. No plows had come down the street yet, and the snow was increasing by the moment.

He closed the door, shaking his head. "It always amazes me how much more snow falls here in the mountains than it did in Colorado Springs."

"We should go before the roads get any worse."

He stepped closer to Rachel. "We should."

She closed the gap even more. "I don't want to go."

"I don't want you to go."

The reluctance on Rachel's face seemed to match his. Given the choice, he would've stayed in his empty family room, kissing Rachel for a very long time. He stepped up close to her and cupped her chin in his hand before placing a soft kiss on her lips. He looked into her eyes for a long moment, hoping she could sense how much he didn't want her to go. "I'll go get our cars started and the snow brushed off them, then I'll carry the kids out."

She gave him a smile that made him want to brave an arctic snowstorm for her, then he gave her one more kiss before he turned to grab their keys.

eleven

RACHEL

RACHEL STARED at the two-page magazine spread that she'd been working on, knowing that something was wrong with it but not being able to focus enough to figure it out. She finally gave up and swiveled in her chair to face Lucy.

"I said yes to being spontaneous on Friday."

Lucy was quick to stop trying new fonts for the image she was working on and turn her full attention to Rachel. "What? You did not."

"I totally did. Remember on Friday how I told you that Aiden and I were going to have a present-wrapping party and then I hoped he'd fall asleep quickly so I could wrap his?"

Lucy nodded.

"Nick called just as I was leaving work to say that

he'd finished with the last project in his new house and wanted to move in on Saturday, so he asked if we could meet to finish that fireplace for Aiden's school program on Friday."

"Based on how distracted you've seemed all day, I'm guessing it went well?"

She hadn't realized she'd been distracted enough for others to notice. She had to get her head in the game... *After* this conversation. She definitely needed to get it all out first. "As much as I had joked about it with Nick that night, it was actually hard! I don't love last-minute plan changes."

"But?"

"But my need to see him very much outweighed my desire to have things scheduled."

"Oh, I wish Court wasn't out of the office today—she would be so freaking proud of you right now, she'd probably have tears in her eyes! Okay, knowing Court, she probably wouldn't. She'd just act all businesslike and give you a 'good job' nod. But *I* have tears in my eyes! This is exactly the kind of thing we were hoping for when we made that bet with you."

Rachel folded her arms. "So, really, the entire bet was so that I would be spontaneous and change my Friday night plans to spend time with a guy?"

Lucy shrugged a shoulder. "Basically."

Rachel chuckled, shaking her head. She should've known.

"So things are going well?"

"Yeah. I really like him." She paused a moment, trying to decide if she wanted to share even though she knew she was going to, whether she offered it on her own or she waited for Lucy to ask. "We kissed."

"And?"

Rachel took a long, slow breath before answering. "I didn't know that kissing him could be so great. Before experiencing Nick's kisses, my brain couldn't even imagine it could be so incredible."

Lucy fanned her face with her hand.

"He was just so sweet! He kissed me like I was so..." She waved her hands, trying to find the words. "Important. Cherished. Like he was simultaneously trying to treat me with such great care, yet completely taking my breath away. The whole night was just the kind that you know you'll remember for the rest of your life." She could hear the longing in her voice, the craving to be near him. Yet, she also felt the uncertainty, and Lucy picked right up on it.

She cocked her head. "Why do I feel like there's a *but* coming?"

Rachel picked up a pen from her desk and started playing with it. "I don't know. It's all just too much. I feel like Aiden and I are busy every second of the day. Relationships just take a lot of time—especially new relationships."

"But it's a good way to spend time, right?"

"It's the best." She sighed just thinking about it. "I told him a couple of weeks ago that my mom used to leave Dove chocolates on my pillow for me and that doves at Christmastime, especially, are special to me. Even though he's been crazy busy all weekend getting moved into his new house, I got to work this morning and when I passed by reception, Shelly said a man dropped something off for me. It was a package of Dove chocolates with a note from Nick that said he hopes I have a peaceful week. How thoughtful is that?"

Rachel leaned back in her chair and looked up toward the ceiling. "We've been staying up late every night talking on the phone for hours after both of our kids have gone to bed. Sometimes he'll just text in the middle of the day to let me know that he's thinking of me." She put her hand over her heart. "It's the sweetest thing, and it just blows me away to know that someone cares about me that much."

"Oh! My heart just melted for you!"

"But do you know how little sleep I've got lately? We've been staying up so late that I completely slept through my alarm this morning."

"That was why you were late?"

She nodded. "And there's just so much to do."

"Is that what you're worried about?" Lucy asked. "Because the busyness isn't going to be an all-the-time thing. It's just crazy right now because Christmas is this week and this is our busy time of year at work. It'll get better."

Rachel looked down at the pen in her hand and then set it on her desk again. "It isn't just that. Friday night, we laid a blanket on the floor of Nick's empty dining room and had dinner sitting down with the kids. I brought cookies—"

"Homemade?"

"Lucy. Remember the part about being busy all the time? No, I didn't make them. Sugarplum Fairy Bakery did."

"Mmm. That's the next best thing."

"Right? So I got cookies, but we didn't eat them with dinner and kind of forgot about them. Then, as we were working, Aiden and Holly asked if they could have one. My immediate thought was no—it was way too close to bedtime and Aiden knew not to ask for something sweet that late at night. But in the spirit of the *Season of Yes*, I would've stopped myself before saying no and said yes. But Nick said yes without even thinking about it first."

"And this is a problem why?"

Rachel blew out a breath, feeling stupid for even bringing it up. "It wasn't a problem. It just did make me think that as much as I've wished over the years that I had a partner in the whole parenting thing and knew how much it would help, it just had somehow not occurred to me that we might not agree on parenting styles and that might be a challenge. The cookie thing wasn't a big deal at all. But it did make me wonder how many things we might run into that might be a bigger deal." It was a fear she hadn't even known she had until Friday night.

"Yeah, I can see how that would be tough."

"So, I'll worry about something like that, then *bam*! I'll get the image in my head of Nick carrying each of the kids, all bundled up in blankets, out to each of our cars as the snow fell softly, the moon and the Christmas lights casting a soft glow on them, then getting them all safe and buckled in. And then I'm just left confused and really *really* wanting him by me, his arms around me, his lips on mine."

"He carried them out to the car? Oh my goodness, I think my heart just melted again. Completely this time. It's now just a puddle."

"But here's where it gets intense. I had read a book to Aiden and Holly. When I was hugging Aiden goodnight, he was acting like he wanted to tell me something so badly that he couldn't hold it in. When we were at the Christmas Village a couple of weeks ago, he had a 'Christmas wish' that he rolled up and put in the claw of a dove. He said, 'I want to tell you what I wished for but I can't say it out loud or it won't come true. So how about I whisper it in your ear?' Do you want to know what he wished for? A dad! And, of course, Holly whispered something to Nick at the same time, and then I saw the two kids share a look."

"Oh, that's sweet."

"I don't know. What if I'm just giving him more false hope than a six-year-old can handle? That's not fair to him. Or Holly. For all I know, she was whispering about what she wanted for breakfast the next day. But if that look that I saw between them was what I think it was, it was conspiratorial. Maybe Holly wants the same thing—a second parent."

Lucy was silent for a long moment before she said, "You say you want to get married and that you want Aiden to have a dad. But do you really?"

"I do!"

"With every other guy you've started to date, you backed away pretty quickly because you didn't think he was good enough for Aiden. Now you find this guy who actually *is* perfect, yet you're still backing away."

Rachel ran her hands over her face. "I know. I don't know what's wrong with me. I'm thirty years old, and I've never had a long-term relationship." She shook her head. "Maybe I just can't handle it."

"You can handle it."

But she wasn't so sure. She didn't have history on her side.

AN AIR of excitement and anticipation filled the gym as Rachel and Nick found seats where they all had a good view of the stage. Maybe it was because the kids only had two more days of school left before Christmas break, or maybe it was just what happened when dozens of parents of first graders got together to see their little ones performing something they had been working so hard on.

Nick reached out and put his hand on hers, and she nearly moaned, right there in the middle of the crowded gym, it felt so good to feel his touch. To have his warm hand on hers, soft as a caress. She was so far gone for this man that it scared her. She forced herself to pay attention as Miss Goodrich got up and thanked everyone for coming and introduced the program.

Then the curtains opened and everyone clapped. She immediately found Aiden with all the other first graders on the risers, Holly right next to him. His eyes were scanning the crowd and as soon as they landed on her and Nick, he started waving wildly. Holly followed Aiden's gaze, and she waved, too, although much more restrained.

As she watched them up on stage, singing the first two songs they'd learned, she couldn't help but think about how much Aiden was falling for Nick, too. As they'd walked into the school, Aiden had held Rachel's hand and Holly held Nick's. Then Aiden had reached out with his other hand and took Nick's free hand, so he was between the two of them. As great as it was, and as much as it had made it feel like they were a little family of four, it freaked her out even more because she could see how much Aiden was getting attached.

When they finished singing the two songs, they started reciting the poem *The Night before Christmas* and she pulled out her phone to video it. It was impressive that they knew it so well—it was a long poem. Aiden had been practicing it at home so much that she all but had the thing memorized, too.

Then they got to the part where they listed the names of the eight reindeer and a couple of kids started saying the names out of order, which messed up more kids, and soon it was all just a jumble of reindeer names. She chuckled, trying to keep it silent so it wouldn't be on the video.

Neither she nor Nick, though, managed to keep their chuckling quiet when Aiden got extra enthusiastic with the line "Now dash away! Dash away! Dash away all," making arm motions that Holly was quick to mimic. The poor kid on the other side of Aiden nearly got knocked off the riser in the exuberance.

Then came the line, "Down the chimney St. Nicholas came with a bound," and the six-year-old who was dressed as Santa took it to mean that he needed to leap through the fireplace opening. The big, stuffed bag that the kid had slung onto his back didn't quite follow the same trajectory, and it hit the side of the set piece.

The kid yanked the bag at the same time, and as the group said in unison, "He was dressed all in fur, from his head to his foot," the fireplace started slowly tipping forward and everyone in the audience leaned in their seats, holding their breaths.

As the falling of the fireplace started to pick up speed, the kids on the risers noticed and all the ones on Aiden's side leaped from their spots and rushed to push it back to standing. Most of the other kids were gasping and pointing, but a handful of kids kept saying the lines of the poem, either oblivious to what was happening or determined to see it through to the end.

They got the fireplace righted and the audience let out a collective breath. The kids were all grinning like they'd singlehandedly saved Christmas.

"Don't worry, Santa," Aiden said, loud enough that everyone heard, "we've got your back."

"Ho, ho, ho," Santa said. "Thank you for saving my life."

"Does this mean we'll get extra presents?" A kid called out.

They were down to three kids still reciting the poem, and as they were very determinedly shouting now, "He had a broad face and a little round belly that shook when he laughed, like a bowl full of jelly."

Besides the three kids determined to finish the poem, chaos erupted. Some were peeking into Santa's bag, Santa was strutting around on the stage, the rescuers of the fireplace were giving each other high fives, and one kid was randomly dancing like no one was watching. The audience was howling with laughter as the three first-grade teachers took to the stage, trying to reestablish order.

It was tough holding the camera steady through her laughter. She glanced over at Nick. He was grinning at the whole display. Then he turned to her as the kids finally got back up on the risers and the volume in the room lessened. "What do you think? Should we head out for an after-program ice cream when this is over? I heard that *With a Cherry on Top* in Nestled Hollow is fantastic."

She was getting better at allowing spontaneity into her schedule, but it still wasn't easy. Studies had shown that kids thrived more on a predictable schedule, and she'd veered off her daily, weekly, and monthly schedules all season long. But a week ago, she would've said yes anyway, just because of the Season of Yes bet.

But today, that wasn't her biggest worry. In fact, her mind was chock full of flat-out fears. She was afraid that she was making a wrong choice and that it would impact all four of them. But more than that, it felt like the choices weren't even all up to her—she was a snowball rolling downhill, picking up size and speed as she went. She couldn't steer or stop and had no choice but to go along with it. It was all out of her control. Saying yes to everything instead of following her trusty plans didn't help.

"I don't think we better," she whispered back. "We've been so busy that Aiden hasn't been getting enough sleep lately, and I don't want him having trouble sleeping tonight, since tomorrow is a school day. And the last two days of school before Christmas break are so crazy—I don't want to add to it."

Nick nodded. "You're right." She didn't miss the disappointed look on his face, though.

She probably had a disappointed look on her face, too. But as much as part of her wanted to say yes to Nick and not care about schedules, the other part of her was completely freaking out and she didn't know how to make it stop. Or if she even should.

twelve

NICK

"OKAY," Nick said as he swiveled around in his office chair and reached for another box. "It sounds like the timeline after the break for the next release is doable." This was his last meeting of the day, on the last day he had to work before he got a full week off for Christmas and New Year's. Maybe with the time off, he'd be able to finally get the last box unpacked.

He had to admit, life was pretty great. He and Holly were settled in their own place again and he was working in his new office. It was good to have an actual space for work. He'd worked at the company office full-time before relocating to Mountain Springs, so transitioning to the folding table in the cramped guest room of his in-laws' home had been tough. But it made him appreciate his new space even more.

Plus, Rachel was in his life. And Aiden was such a cool kid. Holly had her last day of school before the break two days ago, so she was spending the day with his in-laws to help them get ready for the annual Ugly Christmas Sweater party they put on every year. He would get Rachel and Aiden and head over as soon as he was off work.

"Who do we have lined up from the UX team to do the design and layout for it?" he asked as he sliced through the tape holding a box closed. He didn't have to be on camera for this meeting. He didn't even have to be at his computer for it. So he had been wearing his wireless headphones and mic so he could move around while unpacking and organizing his office.

It had been quite a few weeks since he'd packed most of these boxes, and he hadn't thought to label them any more specifically than which room they belonged in. So the contents of each had been a surprise.

"I think it's Andrus."

"Okay, that'll be good. And Mary is confident that we can implement the new features with the current system?"

He pulled out a couple of file folders that hadn't made it into the box with the others that he'd already unpacked as Doug told him about which features the client wanted that would work out just fine and the one that they were still concerned about.

Then he reached in to grab an upside-down wooden box, turned it over, and his breath caught in his throat. It was a shadow box that Clara had made for him right after they'd gotten home from a vacation to the beach— the last vacation they'd taken. A photo was affixed right in the center of the three of them. Clara had her arms around his middle, and he had one arm over her shoulders and held a four-year-old Holly with his other arm. All three of them were grinning.

The rest of the display piece had memorabilia from the nearby museums they'd gone to, shells and colored glass they'd found on the beach, and smaller pictures of the sandcastle they'd built and of the three of them sitting at the edge of the beach where the waves came in, covering their legs. He remembered that vacation like it had just happened. They'd written messages in the sand, watched the sunset, ate lunch right on the beach, and daydreamed for hours.

All the memories came crashing in, just like the waves had, one right after another, and each came with a stab of missing Clara.

"Nick? You still there?"

Nick cleared his throat, trying to also clear out the emotion he was sure would come through loud and clear. "Can we finish discussing this after the break? I'm sorry—I've got to go."

He ended the call, pulled off his headphones, and

stared down at the picture, not even realizing that he had started crying until he felt the tears on his cheeks. Most of the time, he felt like he'd worked through his grief and was doing well. Sometimes he just missed Clara so much it hurt.

And sometimes, like right now, it felt like a wave had come in that was so large it completely submerged him in the ocean water, threatening to pull him out to sea. He ran a hand over his eyes blurred too much to see the picture of the three of them, looking so happy and so oblivious about what their near future held.

From nearly fourteen months of experience, he knew that it didn't work to just push the emotions away when they hit—they were attached to a rubber band and they'd just come back fast and hit so much harder. So he let himself feel the grief of missing someone that he'd loved so much. He let himself cry. He let himself take in that emptiness inside as everything around it felt big and heavy and crushing.

When the tears finally slowed and his ragged breathing turned smooth yet shallow, his neck muscles still tensed from all the emotion they'd been attempting to hold, he started to wonder what in the world he was doing. Clara held so much of his heart. How could he have a relationship with Rachel when he couldn't give her his full heart? It didn't seem fair to her at all.

And how could he have a relationship with a woman

whose cancer could relapse? What if he ever had to go through this again?

He tried to smile at Clara in the picture, but his lips immediately fell again. He sniffed and pressed the heel of his hand over one of his eyes. Then he whispered, "I don't know how to do this, Clara. I know you want me to find someone new and love again, but I don't know what I'm doing."

NICK WALKED up the sidewalk to his in-laws' house with Rachel and Aiden. Holly must've been watching out for them because she opened the door before they even reached it. Welcome," she said, throwing one arm wide, clearly pleased by all the party preparations she'd helped with.

Nick had texted Rachel and then his mother-in-law to let them know that he would be a little late, then he'd jumped in the shower and let the warm water wash away the tears and relax the sore muscles in his neck and shoulders. By the time he'd stepped out and wrapped a towel around his waist, he'd felt so much better. Not one hundred percent—that would take another day or so—but better enough to go to the Christmas party.

"Hey, HollyBear. How was your day?"

"*So* great. Take your coats off and come see!"

As they all took off their coats, he smiled at Rachel's ugly sweater. It was striped, but with a beach scene complete with palm trees and a flamingo, and she'd added little Christmas lights to the trees and around the neck that lit up, fading from one color to the next. He smiled. "They are going to love your sweater."

She grinned. "Thanks! Yours is..." she moved her head around like she was either trying to take it all in or find words to say, "one of the most fascinating things I've ever seen."

He chuckled and took a little bow. A friend from work had sent him the link just after Christmas last year and he'd bought it then, but this was his first time wearing it. It was also striped and looked like someone had tried to shove as many Christmas items on it as possible. A felt gingerbread man, embroidered snowflakes, a string of lights made from shiny colored fabric, tinsel was wrapped around the arms, puffy snow covered the bottom, and a sleigh and eight tiny reindeer flew across the sky. It was the most awful thing he'd ever seen and instantly knew it would be a hit.

"Mine, too?" Aiden said, puffing out his chest. His was a green sweater he'd decorated like a tree with ribbon and pompoms.

"Yours, too," Nick said. "They will all love it."

"I made it myself. Well, my mom did the glue gun part. But it's just like the costume me and my uncle Jack made for Bailey for the pet costume parade last year."

"Everyone loves mine," Holly said. She was growing out of everything so fast that he'd had to get her a new sweater this year. They'd been searching online stores together, and Holly had nearly died of happiness when they'd found a pink one with a decorated tree on it, tipped over, with a dog that looked remarkably like Rosy sitting on top of the tree.

Aiden ran ahead with Holly toward the party where, hopefully, she would introduce him to the other kids. He never wanted to squash any of his daughter's competitiveness, but he did talk to her about being nice and showing Aiden around.

"Come on," he said, putting his hand at the small of Rachel's back. "Let me introduce you to everyone."

They walked through the opening that led to his in-laws' kitchen, dining area, and family room which was fully decked out for Christmas. They'd clearly been baking all day because the place smelled of cinnamon, baked goods, and some kind of savory something that made his stomach growl.

Since they'd arrived a bit late, the place was already filled with people—most were Clara's relatives— standing and chatting, holding little plates of appetizers.

When Tanner spotted them walking into the room, he walked toward him as he called out, "May all your sweaters be ugly and bright! Hey, like yours!" He chuckled and slapped Nick on the back. "Hi, Nick. Good to see you."

"You, too." Nick turned to Rachel. "That's Tanner. He's a cousin."

Then his uncle Roger shouted, "'Tis the season for leftovers and stretchy pants!"

Nick rubbed the back of his neck. "That's... kind of a thing at this party—the random Christmas clichés turned on their sides."

He'd barely finished the sentence when Uncle Ken said loudly, "May your merry be large and your bills be small."

He led Rachel straight over to Ben and Linda for introductions, since they'd been dying to meet her. Just like he'd guessed, they were very welcoming to Rachel. His father-in-law started telling her about how he'd gotten a company to install permanent Christmas lights on his home that could stay there year round and that he could change the colors to match the holiday with his phone, right when Aunt Beverly leaned into his other side and whispered, "Is it appropriate to bring someone new *here*? At a get-together with Clara's family?"

He winced.

"Yes, it is," Linda said in her firm voice that always

sounded like a decision was final. "This is exactly where it's appropriate to bring her."

Uncle Ken was at Aunt Beverly's other side and said, "Don't get your tinsel in a twist, honey."

Linda gave Nick a reassuring smile and he glanced at Rachel, hoping she didn't hear the exchange.

As they walked away from his in-laws, Rachel said, "They're so nice!"

They were. He was relieved that she'd only been hearing what Ben and Linda were saying and not what Aunt Beverly said.

The noise level in the room seemed to rise just then, and Grandpa Hudson said in a loud voice, "Whoever wrote 'All is calm, all is bright,' clearly hasn't been here."

Nick, along with everyone else in the room, held up their drink or their plate of appetizers if they didn't have a drink, and shouted, "Ayy!" Then he turned to Rachel. "We do this every time grandpa quotes any lines from *Silent Night*. It's... kind of like a drinking game, I guess." He remembered the first time he was introduced to this group—Rachel probably thought they were as weird and eccentric as he had. She just chuckled, though.

"Who is this?" Uncle Pete said as he walked up to Rachel and Nick.

"This is Rachel Meadows, the woman I've been dating. Rachel, this is Uncle Pete."

Uncle Pete pulled his head back a little. "Oh. I didn't

think you'd be starting to date again already." Then, in a hesitant voice that conveyed how much he didn't mean what he said, he added, "Good job."

"I wasn't sure I would be, either." Nick smiled at Rachel as he slipped an arm around her waist. "Life surprises you sometimes." He hoped that Uncle Pete would get the hint not to push it any further and he hoped that Rachel would get the message that he was there for her regardless of anything anyone said.

Ken called out, "Santa Claus has the right idea to only see people once a year," and everyone laughed.

They had barely turned away from Uncle Pete when Tanner's wife, Tiff, put her hand on Nick's arm, giving him a face full of pity. "How are you, Nick?"

"I'm good. Tiff, this is Rachel, Rachel, Tiff."

Tiff smiled at Rachel and then turned back to Nick. "I'm glad you're doing well. Oh, I just miss Clara so much! I was telling Tanner that if he died young, I don't think I'd *ever* be ready to date again."

"It's definitely tough, but I bet you'd get there if you were ever faced with that situation." What was he thinking, bringing Rachel to a family event put on by Clara's parents, where so many of Clara's relatives would be present, when he and Rachel had only been together for a short time?

He was probably thinking everyone would be like

Clara's parents—super supportive of him dating again. He hadn't been prepared for this. He was especially ill-prepared after the emotionally draining afternoon he'd had.

They made the rounds to almost everyone in the group, and it was probably getting close to the games starting when a group of kids ran by Grandpa Harold, who was now leaning back in an armchair with his eyes closed. "I'm not 'sleeping in heavenly peace' here."

"Ayy," everyone called out as they held up whatever was in their hands. Rachel did this time, too.

Aiden came to stop in front of Rachel, so she crouched down to his height as he said, "There's someone whose sweater is like a fireplace, when they put their arms out straight like this, stockings are hanging down from it! Also, can you believe Christmas is in *two days*? And guess what? I told Holly's grandma that hanai means family that's kind of related but not really. Then I asked, and she said I could be her hanai, but Holly said it was only okay if Noelle's mom could also be *her* hanai. Do you think Grandma Allred would be okay with that?"

Rachel glanced at Nick before meeting Aiden's eyes again. "I bet she would."

Nick hadn't had time to process all that before his elderly Aunt Virginia pulled him toward her and patted his arm. "Are you sure you're ready to start dating again, dear?"

He took a deep breath.

"Because, you know, grief can come along and strike you at any moment."

Yep. He knew that all too well. It hit him earlier today and was hitting him pretty hard right now.

"Everyone encouraged me to start dating again a few years after Frank died," Aunt Virginia said. "So eventually, I said "Fine!" and I went on a date with a nice gentleman. The whole time I felt like I was cheating on Frank, and I kept looking around the restaurant like I was going to get caught for stepping out on him. There was just so much guilt. So I said 'I'm done.' It just wasn't worth it. I decided that I'm going to be true to my Frank always. To death, just like I said in my vows."

If that wasn't a truckload of guilt being dumped on him, he didn't know what was. He glanced over at Rachel, who was talking with Uncle Ken. He hoped she was faring better than he was.

Aunt Virginia patted his arm again. "When Clara married you and you two chose to have a child, she was choosing *you* to be Holly's dad. She didn't choose *someone else* to be Holly's mom. How would you even know if she approved of this person? Because if you find someone new, she'll be Holly's mom."

Knowing Aunt Virginia, she wasn't intentionally trying to be hurtful; he knew that, but all her words were like swords nonetheless. He took a steadying breath and said, "Clara would trust me to find the perfect person. And she would approve of Rachel."

"Hello, Virginia," his father-in-law said. "I apologize for interrupting, but can I steal Nick away from you? I need his help."

Aunt Virginia patted his arm one last time and then turned away to talk to someone else. Nick let out a long, slow breath before turning to Ben. "What did you need help with?"

"Nothing. It just looked like that wasn't the most pleasant of conversations for you, and I know Virginia will talk your ear off if given the chance."

He clapped his father-in-law on the back. "You're a good man, Ben. Thank you." He was truly grateful. He wasn't sure he could've taken many more stabs from Aunt Virginia.

Ben smiled, and then said, "Now go be with your date."

When Nick reached Rachel, he was met with a smile that faded just a bit when she took in whatever was on his face. "Are you okay?" she asked.

He said "Yes," but she was still looking at him like she could tell that something was wrong. He ran his hands over his face to try to wipe away all of it. "I'll be fine."

And he would be. After such an emotional afternoon, his nerves were just frayed because everyone was saying out loud all the fears he'd been trying to hold inside.

thirteen

RACHEL

RACHEL WAS SO glad that the Allred family had welcomed her and Aiden into their family right along with Jack because their home had become her favorite place to spend Christmas Eve. They had vaulted ceilings and a giant, gorgeously decorated Christmas tree, every area was decked out with garlands and red ornaments, a gingerbread train was moving through a mini village on a table, the long tables separating the kitchen from the family room were adorned in reds and whites with greenery down the middles, and Christmas music played over the speakers.

And this year, instead of being too sick to help, she was right in the middle of the action, cutting up vegetables with her new sister-in-law, Noelle, and Noelle's sister, Katie. She glanced over at Katie's date, who was chatting with one of Noelle's brothers-in-law, who was holding a two-year-old. "The guy you brought is pretty cute. How are things going with the two of you?"

Katie smiled as she glanced up from the cutting board to her date. "They're going fine. I mean he's not 'the one' or anything, but he's still a fun boyfriend. I don't know how much longer it's going to last, but I'm going to enjoy the relationship for as long as it's good."

Noelle, who was wearing a Santa hat with the words *Birthday Girl* stitched into it picked up a baby carrot and asked "What's he missing?" before taking a bite of it.

"I don't know," Katie said. "I'm just waiting for the guy who will just kind of grab me by the heart, you know?"

Rachel hadn't realized it until Katie said it, but that was what she'd been waiting for, too. And Nick had totally grabbed her by the heart. If only her stomach hadn't also been doing what it had been doing this week.

"How are things with you and Nick?" Katie asked.

Rachel lifted a shoulder in a shrug as she sliced the ends off some Brussels sprouts. "Nick is great. It's just that I've been feeling like a snowball rolling downhill, unable to control the speed or the direction, and after last night, it's like I rolled right off a cliff."

"What happened last night?" Noelle asked.

Rachel kept cutting the ends off the Brussels sprouts and slicing them in half. "I have daily, weekly, and monthly plans so everything will stay on schedule and be predictable and nothing will get forgotten, but I haven't been going off them much lately. Last night, after Nick's family party—well, his late wife's family, really—I went into my plans and they were all over the place. Nothing was right, everything was crazy, and it was a total mess. It made me feel even less in control of everything."

"I don't understand," Katie said as she pushed the cut cauliflower from the cutting board into the bowl. "Why did you even go look at it all if things were going fine? Why not just roll with it?"

Rachel hadn't been good at just "rolling with it" in her entire life. She thrived on plans. "Probably because I was trying to regain some control. Or maybe because of everything that happened at the party. Or a combination of both."

She glanced past the dinner tables to where Nick was playing in the family room with all the little kids, fully out of earshot. She let out a big breath and put down the knife, turning to face both Katie and Noelle. "People made so many comments about Nick and me dating last night. I mean, of course, they would—they were Clara's family, and I was just the person trying to fill her shoes. A lot of them were trying to be supportive, I could tell, but underneath, it was like they just knew that I would never be able to take Clara's spot."

And then she voiced the concern that had been growing over the past few days. "What if it's the same way with Nick? From everything I've seen, he and Clara had a great relationship and he really loved her. What if he feels like I could never take her place and he always wishes I was more like her? And what if he isn't even ready for a new relationship? It's only been fourteen months since his wife passed away. If I had a husband die, I don't know that I'd be ready to date again after just that long."

"Men get ready for a new relationship after a spouse dies more quickly than women do," Katie said.

"Really?"

Katie nodded. "Scientific fact." She pointed at Noelle. "Just like Uncle Jim."

"True," Noelle said. "He started dating like what? Five months after Aunt Tracy died? But it had been four *years* since Tracy's husband had passed, and Uncle Jim had been her first date since." She turned to Rachel. "But everyone is different. Fourteen months might be all Nick needed."

"Maybe," she said, but the worry was still there. "Look how attached Aiden has gotten to Nick."

All three of them looked over to where Nick was on the floor, kind of wrestling with all the little kids, all of them piling on top of him. The Allreds' black lab, Captain, was getting in on the fun, too.

"Oh my goodness, that is the sweetest," Noelle said.

They all just watched him. It really was the sweetest, seeing him have so much fun with the kids and they have so much fun with him. She loved that he was so willing to get on the floor with them. She had plenty of worries in her stomach, but the scene warmed her heart. He had been on his hands and knees, but then raised his torso, still on his knees, arms in the air, and growled. All the little kids squealed and then laughed.

Then Aiden went up to him, wrapped his arms around Nick's neck, and gave him a tight hug. Nick's eyes instantly found hers and she could see in that expression that he was worried about Aiden getting so attached, too, which only validated her worries.

"I'm so sorry to dump all of this on you two," she said. "And it's your birthday, Noelle! And Christmas Eve!"

Nick stood up, peeled a couple of kids off his legs, said something to them that made them all laugh, and then headed in her direction. Jack opened the last folding chair he'd brought up and came over, too, and both men joined them at the same time. Jack kissed Noelle on her cheek.

"Are you so excited to leave for your honeymoon tomorrow?" Katie asked

"Cancun!" Noelle said. "I can't wait!"

Rachel was so grateful that both women changed the subject so effortlessly.

"Thanks again for letting us stay at your house tonight," Jack said. "We're pretty excited."

Rachel nodded. "I've got the air mattress all set up for you in the living room. It's definitely worth getting excited over."

"I'm just glad that we can stay here as long as we'd like without having to think about making the drive back to Golden tonight," Noelle said. "Oh, and we just heard—our house should be ready for us to move in the day before we return from our honeymoon."

Jack smiled at her and Rachel soaked in how happy she was for her brother to have found someone that made him smile like that. "Remember when we were here a year ago?" he asked.

Noelle nodded. "It was the night that everything changed." They looked at each other with such love before they shared a quick kiss.

Rachel looked up at Nick, who had slid in right beside her, and got a sinking in the pit of her stomach, making her wonder if tonight might be the night that everything was going to change for them, too.

"Happy birthday to Noelle," Aiden called out.

Everyone shouted in return, "And to Noelle a good night!"

Aiden giggled even more than he had when they had

shouted the same phrases last year. Probably because now he knew that its inspiration came from the poem his class had memorized.

As soon as the last item came out of the oven, Mr. Allred announced that dinner was ready and they all took their seats along the long row of tables.

All through the dinner, it just felt like something was off between her and Nick, but she couldn't decipher how much of it was coming from her and how much of it was coming from him. All she knew was that it wasn't only her, and it made her stomach hurt enough that she was struggling to make it look like she didn't hate all the food on her plate. She knew from last year that every item was delicious—she just couldn't eat it today.

Then Holly said, "Grandma, can you please pass the stuffed mushrooms?"

Rachel could tell by the way Nick stiffened when he heard evidence that his daughter had claimed this family as her own that he was worried about her attachment to them. And the only way he'd be worried about that was if he didn't think their relationship was going to work out. Nick must've felt her attention on him, because he started to turn her direction, but not enough to make eye contact before glancing away.

She desperately wished that they weren't in a room with nearly two dozen people so she could just have a conversation with Nick and understand where his thoughts were. She always felt such a calm, peaceful feeling around him, and if they could talk, she knew she'd get that back.

If she hadn't thought that things were off before, she would've known they were when they sat with the Allred family to watch the Christmas Eve video that Katie made. Instead of putting an arm around her once they sat on the couch so she could snuggle into him like he would've done even just a couple of days ago, he sat stiffly next to her, his hands in his lap.

She was sure the video was great—especially with all the laughing and wiping of tears everyone around her was doing—but she was struggling to pay attention to it. She couldn't pretend that things were okay with her and Nick and she couldn't wait any longer to ask him about it. Leaning in close, she whispered, "Do you want to meet me in the living room to talk?"

He nodded, so she turned to Aiden on her other side and whispered, "I'll be right back." He was having so much fun with the other kids his age that he probably wouldn't even notice that she was gone.

Once in the living room, she looked at Nick for a moment as they stood next to the smaller tree that was right in front of the Allreds' front window. She immediately thought of that first day she'd met him when she'd gone to meet with Aiden's teacher about making the fireplace set piece. He still stood tall, showing off that great build, his auburn hair with the perfect amount of curl. She remembered thinking back then that his eyes were the color of the sea on a cloudy day, and now there was a storm of emotion going on behind them.

"You seem to have a lot on your mind." She did, too. Well, actually, she had a lot more going on in her gut. "Do you want to talk about it?"

He drew in a deep breath and shook his head as he glanced back in the direction of the family room, like he didn't want to talk about anything there. Or maybe he just didn't want to talk about it on Christmas Eve. But maybe he couldn't pretend any longer that everything was okay, either, because he gave a slight nod.

He put his hands in his pockets, and she wondered if he maybe didn't quite know what to say. She understood —everything she'd been feeling over the past few days was a jumble in her mind, too. A jumble of fears that were more intense now than they'd ever been. As intense as she was feeling everything, though, the look on his face told her that maybe he was feeling it more.

He reached a hand forward like maybe he was going to take her hand in his, but then decided against it and instead ran the hand over his face. "I am so new at all of this—trying to date again after Clara. And I don't know what I'm doing. I don't even know that I *can* do this. I kind of jumped in too quickly and didn't anticipate or think things through enough."

He paced over toward the window and then turned around to face her again. "I didn't know how I would feel about dating again until I did it. And now that I have, I'm not sure about anything. And I really didn't think about how everything would affect Holly—I was just happy that my daughter was making friends. I hadn't thought through far enough about what would happen if..."

He let the sentence trail off like he wasn't sure he wanted to say the words out loud. So she did. "If things with us didn't work out?"

He looked into her eyes for a long moment, and she felt so many things pass between them so quickly that she couldn't interpret any of them. "Yeah."

Rachel swallowed hard, the weight in her stomach feeling like it was doubling even as she started to think her next words. She said them anyway. "I've been worried about the same thing. Maybe..." She trailed off, and then just decided she should plow ahead, letting that fear that had been building up so strongly inside her take the wheel. It wasn't something she could contain much longer, anyway. "Maybe we should back away before things go any further."

He hesitated, his mouth parted like he was going to say something. His eyes searched hers, and she could see in his just what it was doing to him. How much this was destroying him. But then he brought his lips together and nodded once in agreement.

She stood frozen, just staring at Nick as the noise level in the family room rose. The video had probably finished. Had she really just ended things with Nick? Had he? Had they both decided that it was over? That this was the best thing? She felt a tear run down her cheek and she reached up to brush it away, knowing there were many more behind it, yet also knowing that they couldn't come yet.

The expression on Nick's face as she felt everything inside her crumble nearly undid her. His eyes were soft, his forehead furrowed in concern, his lips pulled down. At first, she thought in sadness, and then she realized it was the look of devastation. They should've realized all the reasons why their relationship wouldn't work earlier and ended things long ago. Before their hearts got in so deep that an ending would break them.

Jingle bells sounded just outside the house and the noise in the family room rose even more, mostly from the kids. Still, though, she didn't take her eyes off Nick until Aiden and Holly raced into the room.

"Mom!" Aiden shouted, grabbing her hand. "We have to get home and get to sleep super quickly!"

"Santa is almost here!" Holly said, grabbing Nick's hand and pulling him toward the couch that held their coats as Aiden pulled Rachel toward the family room, where she'd left her things.

She kept her eyes on Nick for as long as she could, feeling that as they were being pulled apart, he was taking her heart with him.

fourteen

NICK

A GUST of wind hit Nick as he and Holly stepped out of the Allreds' home, biting into him, making him hunch his shoulders to bring his coat closer to his ears. He felt Holly shiver through the hand he held. There was already frost on his car—he wished he would've started it ahead of time so it could have been warming up.

There were a lot of things he wished he would've done differently tonight. He started the car as Holly got in, then he grabbed the blanket in the back seat and spread it over her so she wouldn't freeze. After grabbing the ice scraper from the trunk, he went to work on the windows. The lump in his throat felt as big as the one in his gut, and his mind was a blizzard of thoughts and emotions.

He'd had doubts about having a relationship that had wound their way into his mind for quite a few days. The inner turmoil that had started with hearing about Rachel's cancer, elevated when he'd found the shadowbox Clara had made, and continued through the ugly sweater party and the Christmas Eve dinner was huge. He thought that by ending things with Rachel he'd feel relief from that turmoil. That it would be stopping it at the source.

So why did he feel so much worse now? His guts ached. His heart was filled with regrets and pangs of loneliness. His head was a clouded mess where nothing felt right. In fact, that it couldn't be more wrong.

He shook the ice off the scraper and tossed it back into his trunk before getting into his car, rubbing his hands together to give them a little warmth before grabbing the steering wheel. The entire ride home, Holly was chatting a million miles an hour about Christmas.

"This whole time, I figured I was on Santa's nice list, because I've been trying super hard to be nice to people, but as you were scraping the windows, Daddy, I suddenly wondered when Santa downloads the list."

"Downloads the list?"

"Yeah, you know, so he can print it out and give it to the elves so they can get everything ready to go. Did he download it like a month ago so they'd have plenty of time? Because a month ago, I'm not sure I was on the nice list. Do you think I'm going to wake up tomorrow and there's just going to be underwear under the tree? Because Zach S. said that one year he was pretty sure he was on the naughty list and he didn't get coal—he got underwear."

"I don't think Santa has a naughty and nice list. I think he just loves when you keep trying."

"Really? *Phew.* There are a lot of kids in my class who will be relieved to hear that. Hey, does Santa have any kids? Or are the elves like his kids?" Holly had been trying to get a satisfactory answer to that one for days.

The questions went on and on, and he did his best to answer each one, wondering how she was ever going to relax enough to fall asleep tonight.

As soon as they stepped through the garage door into the house, Rosy greeted them with as much excitement and lack of tiredness as Holly had been showing. Bedtime was sure to be rough tonight.

He went through all the motions with Holly, trying to keep a smile on his face the whole time. They placed a glass of milk and the package of Reese's Peanut Butter Cups they'd gotten for Santa on the table. When they'd last been at the store, Holly had decided that Santa was definitely a dad and that dads liked Reese's (based solely on the fact that Nick did), so they should get him that instead of cookies.

Finally, he got both the dog and his daughter tucked

into bed. He pulled the blankets up to her chin and gave her a kiss on the forehead. "Goodnight, Hollyberry."

"Goodnight, Daddy. Since this is the night before Christmas, I'm going to have visions of sugar plums dancing in my head."

He chuckled. "I can't wait to hear about it tomorrow."

"And I can't wait to go to eat cinnamon rolls at Aiden's tomorrow after we open presents."

The weight in his stomach somehow got heavier. "Actually, we are going to celebrate at home tomorrow until we go to Grandma's and Grandpa's."

She sat up in bed. "What? But no. I really want to go see Aiden and Rachel!"

"Don't worry," he said as she lay back down and he fixed her blankets again, "I'm going to make it a super special morning." He had no idea how. Making it more special than being there with Rachel and Aiden felt like an impossible task. Sometime tomorrow he'd have to share the reason why they weren't going there in the morning, once he figured out how to do that.

After he left Holly's room, pulling the door closed behind him, he wandered through his house. He'd been so happy to finally have the place finished so they could move in after being in cramped bedrooms at his in-laws. He had so much space now, but instead of feeling spacious, it just felt... empty.

He couldn't believe that he'd ended things with Rachel. Or more that he went along with her ending things without him doing a single thing to fight for the relationship. He'd felt so much turmoil leading up to tonight, but now all he could think of was everything he'd loved about being with Rachel over the past several weeks. How much he loved talking with her, texting her, doing things together with the kids, and spending time with just her.

Every memory he had with her was perfect, which made the pang of losing something that had the potential to be so great even more painful. What were the chances of a guy getting the opportunity to fall completely in love twice in his lifetime? He had it. And he threw it all away. He was feeling the pain of that loss acutely.

After mindless wandering through empty rooms, feeling as alone as he had in those first days after Clara died, he checked in on Holly. The excitement of the day must've finally caught up with her because she was fast asleep. He carried the box of presents from his room upstairs to the family room downstairs and put them under the tree.

Then he headed back upstairs, flopped down on his bed, and pulled out his phone. He swiped to the last screen, looked at Clara's face, and said, "Remember a few years ago when I was working at GilsonTech but then got offered a job at Improvementally? I didn't want to accept it, because I was perfectly happy at my job and the new job was such an unknown. I'd been afraid to take it because what if things went badly at the new job? It hadn't felt worth the risk. But you told me that you knew it was a good fit for me and that I would thrive at the new job."

He nodded. "And you were right. It was a very good change for me in so many ways. I never would've been able to work remotely and move here with the old job, either. I've definitely thrived at Improvementally."

He let out a huff of a humorless chuckle and shook his head, then closed his eyes for a moment before facing her picture again. "Apparently, I didn't learn that lesson enough the first time around and needed it again. Except for this time, I didn't choose so well. I think I messed up pretty big, actually." He looked up at the ceiling. "But everything's changed since you died, Clara, and I don't know anymore if I even can make the right choice."

He was just talking to a picture on a phone, yet he still felt bad that he was dumping that all on her. But if she was able to tune in from heaven, he knew she'd understand. He just wished she could also tell him what to do because right now, he didn't know.

fifteen
RACHEL

"MOMMY!" Aiden said as he shook her arm. "Wake up—Santa came!"

"What time is it?" she asked as she pried her puffy eyes open and grabbed her phone. 6:13. It could've been so much worse. "Okay, buddy, I'm getting up. Are Jack and Noelle awake?"

"Yep! I went in and sat on their air mattress before I came in here. It bounced them so much that Noelle nearly fell off her side."

They probably loved that. She rolled out of bed and put on her slippers and bathrobe and headed into the living room. Jack and Noelle were looking as bleary-eyed as she felt, but they wore smiles on their faces.

Last night, after she'd left the Allreds' house, gotten Aiden to bed, made sure Jack and Noelle had everything they needed, and put Christmas presents out, she headed into her room to work on her Monthly Plan. Normally, she would have next year's Yearly Plan done by now, but she couldn't face it yet. The Monthly Plan, though—that, she could do.

She'd gotten the rest of December and all of January planned out. All the appointments in, reminders to do everything, and scheduling when she was going to spend time working on the goals she had for the month. As she'd worked, she'd heard the buzz of Jack and Noelle talking through the wall that she shared with the living room. It was nice. But it also made her long for someone to talk the night away with.

But she had a plan, and she stayed focused on it. Even when the buzz of talking quieted and the hour got later and later. It had felt like it was worth it, though, because she got everything in her planner all nice and neat and exactly how she liked it. Scheduled. Predictable. Deliberate.

The plan had gotten to be such a mess since Nick had stepped into her life. She'd fixed most of December's a few days ago, but it still needed help. So did the entirety of January. Scheduling everything always made her feel better, and since the craziness in her life was one of the reasons why she felt like she should end things with Nick, she figured that boost of energy and happiness that it normally gave her would be doubled.

But it wasn't. All it did was make her feel like everything was wrong without Nick in her life. And it made her get not nearly enough sleep. The two things did not combine well.

She gave her brother and his new wife a sleepy "Good morning," then took Bailey out back to do her morning duties. As she stood, shivering in the cold, she tried to keep herself from thinking about Nick and what happened last night. She had already cried herself to sleep about it and the slightest bit of thinking about it threatened to bring it on again. The puffy eyes weren't helping with the *no-sleep* look she was sporting.

But she did manage to hold things together as they all opened Christmas presents. Jack may have been a Grinch who hated Christmas up until last year, but she hadn't spent a single Christmas morning without him since the year he was born, and she was glad he was there with them. It made her house feel less lonely, too.

Every time, though, that Jack brushed Noelle's cheek with his knuckle, or she snuggled right into him, or he whispered something in her ear that made her laugh, or she smiled at him like he was her whole world, Rachel felt Nick's absence even more intensely.

As she could have guessed, it wasn't the toys that Aiden opened that he loved the most—it was the ream of white printer paper and the new set of markers that had lit up his face the most. The best part was watching him wrap his arms around them, giving them an uncomfortable-looking hug, his expression blissful.

The worst part was seeing two presents left under the tree when they were done unwrapping all of them. One for Nick and one for Holly.

"Who's ready for cinnamon rolls?" she said as she stood from the couch, ready to get some distance between her and the things threatening to make her lose her grip on her emotions.

Aiden, Jack, Noelle, and the dog all joined her by the kitchen counter, Bailey looking just as excited for food as everyone else. Rachel dished up a cinnamon roll for each of them, and as everyone sat down at her little kitchen table, she started getting the dog's food. "When do you need to leave for the airport?"

Jack looked at his watch. "Wow—it got late! We better go get the last of our things packed in the next five minutes, because we need to have the luggage in the car and pulling away in fifteen."

Rachel managed to keep a smile on her face and be happy to see them off on their honeymoon. They were on their way to a warm beach where they were going to be able to just relax and enjoy every minute together, and she was thrilled for them.

As soon as they were off, though, she and Aiden headed back to the kitchen for the cinnamon rolls. Aiden slid into his seat and asked, "Why aren't Nick and

Holly here yet? I thought they were going to have cinnamon rolls with us."

She couldn't believe that she hadn't thought to tell Aiden about the change in plans. "Oh, honey. I'm so sorry I didn't tell you earlier, but they're not coming. Nick and I decided to not see each other anymore."

"What?" Aiden slid off his seat to stand. "But my Christmas wish that I gave to the dove was for a dad! I thought it was going to be Nick. This is the opposite of the wish coming true!"

And then he was crying and she was crying and trying to comfort him and they both were a mess. Rachel couldn't remember the last time she'd cried so much in a twelve-hour period before and it hurt her heart even more that it was hurting Aiden's heart, too.

She was the mom, though, so she couldn't keep being a mess. She needed to pull herself together. "It's still Christmas, and we still have a lot of fun that needs to be had. What do you say we open that Lego set that Uncle Jack and Aunt Noelle got you and see what we can make?"

It was a good distraction for Aiden, but not so effective for her. She couldn't seem to get herself to stop thinking of Nick. She had spent the entirety of adulthood without a man in her life—she knew exactly how to do that. So why did the prospect of spending her life without Nick feel so profoundly sad? She'd never felt such an intense yearning to have someone in her life before.

It wasn't until she no longer had it that she realized it was something she'd been longing for all along—she just hadn't known she needed it. Or wanted it. Or would miss it so much when it was gone. She had been on her own for a long time. She'd been alone in raising Aiden. But she'd never felt lonely—she and Aiden had always been enough, just the two of them. So why did she feel so lonely now?

She told herself that it was because no matter how much Jack had hated Christmas most of his life, they'd always spent the entire day of Christmas together. And right now, she had no family with her outside of Aiden. Her sister-in-law, who had become one of her best friends, was with Jack, on her way to a trip of a lifetime. And her other two best friends weren't even in the state. Courtney was in Oregon and Lucy was in Nebraska, spending Christmas with their families. Her own little family felt so small.

But she knew that the loneliness she was feeling wasn't just because Jack or Noelle or her friends weren't there. It was because over the past few weeks, her family had felt twice as big with Nick, Holly, and Rosy with them.

But mostly, it was because of Nick. She missed him more than she ever fathomed that she could.

sixteen

NICK HAD BEEN SPENDING Christmas Day trying to make it happy for Holly, especially during the morning hours when they were supposed to go to Rachel's for cinnamon rolls. It had occupied him enough, apparently, that he'd completely forgotten that his in-laws were coming over until the doorbell rang.

He answered the door, still wearing his Christmas pajama pants and a t-shirt. As soon as it was open, Rosy raced to the door, and Linda said, "Well, hello, lassie-dog! I am happy to see you, too!" Then she looked up from where she was crouched giving Rosie a neck rub, to see Nick's face. Whatever she saw there made her ask, "What's wrong? Is Holly okay?"

Holly appeared around the corner just then, looking all chipper and running toward them, saying,

"Grandma! Grandpa!" and Linda breathed a sigh of relief.

After she hugged her granddaughter, she stood up straight and turned her attention to Nick. She only studied him for a moment and didn't even ask any questions before she said, "Oh, Nick. I'm so sorry."

Did his expression make it that obvious?

"Goodness, I forgot that I wanted to bring over that treat we got for Nick. How about Holly and I walk back to the house to get it."

Ben's brow furrowed. "Why don't you just give it to him when they come to our house for Christmas dinner in a bit?"

"Dear, I think we need it now." She said, putting extra emphasis on each word.

"Okay. Want me to walk back with you?"

"No, you two stay here." Ben still looked confused, so she added in a whisper that was nearly loud enough for Holly to hear, "Nick and Rachel's relationship took a hit and he needs you to talk to him."

Ben's eyes immediately flew to Nick. "I'm sorry to hear that, son." Then he turned back to his wife. "When did he tell you?"

"Oh, *Ben*, just go talk to him. Grab your coat, Holly—we're about to go on a Christmas wonderland walk!"

As soon as they were both out the door with a very excited Rosy following along, Nick and Ben headed back to his kitchen, family room, and dining area. Nick leaned against the granite countertop of his island and his father-in-law leaned against the table. They both just stood there for a moment, arms crossed, feeling awkward, looking at one another.

"So you two ended things?"

Nick nodded. "Last night."

"What happened?"

"Nothing that should've happened."

"Things didn't go so well with the woman I dated after my first wife died, either. You're new at this dating-after-having-been-married thing. You don't just automatically know what you're doing, and you're bound to make mistakes. It's not the end of the world."

"Well, I definitely made mistakes. But it was more than that." He tried to think about the events of the night before and look at them as a whole so he could figure out what went wrong. After a long moment where Ben just stayed patiently quiet, Nick said, "I think I was scared." He swallowed. "Maybe I still am."

That was so hard to admit, especially to his father-in-law, and it made heat rise to the back of his neck.

But Ben just nodded, like he understood and wasn't judging. So Nick just stayed silent and willed himself not to feel ashamed of the emotion.

"Let's talk about what you are afraid of."

"My dad was in the military, Ben. We didn't grow up

talking about things we were afraid of—we just talked about being brave."

"All right, then," Ben said. "Be brave and tell me what you're afraid of."

Nick shook his head and let out a breath of a chuckle. Then he ran his hand through his hair as he tried to think about what it was, exactly, that he feared.

"I guess I'm afraid of not knowing how to do this. To love someone new. And I'm scared that loving Rachel will..." He wasn't quite sure how to word what he was feeling. "I don't know—diminish what I had with Clara, I guess. Or that I won't be able to give my whole heart to Rachel, and she deserves my all."

His father-in-law stayed quiet for a few moments before he said, "When you love someone, you don't give a piece of your heart to them, a piece to the next person, a piece to the next. You don't have to get the pieces back to give all of it to someone—Rachel and Clara don't have to share your heart. You can love Rachel with your entire heart just like you loved Clara with your entire heart."

Could he?

"I mean, think about when Holly was born. Loving her didn't make you love Clara any less, did it?"

Nick shook his head. "It made me love her even more."

"So why would loving Rachel be any different?"

He hadn't thought about it like that. Could he honor his late wife's memory and still give his entire heart to Rachel?

"Or loving Aiden? Because loving Rachel and wanting a life with her would mean gaining a son and loving him as much as you love your daughter."

Nick nodded as he thought through everything. Before that moment when he'd let fear take hold, he'd felt like he was giving his whole heart to Rachel. It hadn't felt weird or wrong or impossible—it had felt right. Loving Aiden had felt right, too.

But there was something else that had worried him just under the surface for a while now. "Rachel went through cancer treatments recently. Her scan showed no cancer six months ago..."

"But you know she's not in the clear until she's had five years of clean scans."

Nick nodded.

"And you don't know if you can face the possibility of losing another woman you love."

Nick nodded again, not trusting his voice.

"Does Rachel seem very worried about relapsing?"

"I don't think so."

"That's a good sign." Ben was quiet for a long moment before he said, "Here's the thing about life. How long we've got here is an unknown. Someone who's terribly sick can recover and live a long life. And someone who seems healthy in every way—like Clara did—can leave at much too young of an age. It's a risk you take anytime you give your heart to someone."

Could he handle that risk?

"If you knew clear back when you'd first found yourself falling in love with Clara that she would pass away so young, would you have given up having that relationship with her?"

Their entire relationship seemed to fill Nick's mind. Their dating, falling in love, getting engaged, getting married, having Holly, buying their first house, job changes, all the time falling more and more in love. It gave him physical pain just trying to imagine that none of that happened. "No. There's no way I would give that up."

"I didn't think so," Ben said. "Here's another big question for you. Do you think Clara would have an issue with you loving Rachel?"

"No." He was sure of that. Last night, he'd "video chatted" with Clara, and then basically hung up on her after telling her his woes. It wasn't until this morning before he thought about what Clara might think of all of this if she'd been able to talk to him. And the overwhelming feeling he got was that he had her blessing and that she was happy he and Holly wouldn't be alone. He'd almost felt the breath of relief from Clara that he and Holly were loved and had someone to love.

"That's one thing my little girl always had—the ability to want for others even things she couldn't have for herself." He nodded. "I think she'd be proud of you."

Nick swallowed hard and blinked a few times to clear away the emotion that swelled up.

"And I think she'd want you to fight for Rachel."

seventeen

RACHEL

RACHEL PULLED out her phone and sent a message in the group text with Courtney and Lucy.

> Rachel: I said yes to something really bad.

> Courtney: Oh, no. Spill.

> Rachel: I ended things with Nick.

> Lucy: Rachel! I wish I was there instead of being in stupid Nebraska with family so I could hug you!

> Lucy: Just kidding— Nebraska isn't stupid and seeing family is great. But I wish I could be there! Why? Why would you end it?

Courtney: I think we need an emergency meeting via video call. Are you both free?

Rachel looked over to where Aiden and Bailey were wrestling on the floor and knew that they would keep each other occupied for a good ten or fifteen minutes, so she texted back *Yes*. Less than a minute later, she saw two of her best friends' faces on the phone. So she gave them a recap of everything.

"Did this all happen because of the Season of Yes?" Lucy asked.

Rachel shrugged. "I'll admit, that has been really hard."

"Why?" Lucy asked.

"I think just because I like having a schedule."

"But *why* do you? Courtney pressed. "Why does it matter so much to you?"

Rachel looked up, trying to think about why it was hard for her to not have one. "I don't know. I think because it's scary to not have one. Like if I don't, then everything will fall apart. A schedule was how I kept everything steady and consistent for me and Jack when we were kids living in an unpredictable environment. And then, as a mom, I know that it takes a good schedule and a lot of consistency if I want Aiden to thrive."

"Okay," Courtney said, "let's play a game of Worst

Case Scenario. Let's say your schedule gets unpredictable for a bit. What would happen?"

"More frequent meltdowns, for one."

"For you or Aiden?" Lucy asked.

Rachel laughed. "I was thinking Aiden, but now that you mention it..."

"And do you think you would keep it so inconsistent over time?" Courtney said. "Is that in your personality?"

Rachel thought back to the months she went through cancer treatment. Her schedule was as inconsistent as it had ever been then. And it *was* super hard on Aiden. But as soon as she got feeling better again, she was quick to get things back to that steadiness that she always craved. It wasn't just for him—she needed it, too. "No. It would only be short term." Just saying the words gave her a lot of comfort.

"Yes," Courtney said, "a new relationship can throw a monkey wrench in your schedule, but that won't be forever. And you and Aiden will bounce right back."

She nodded, completely believing Courtney's words.

"Yep," Lucy said. "Everything is not going to fall apart. When Courtney and I suggested that you read that book and then we both decided to make the Season of Yes bet with you, what we had in mind was you saying yes to things outside of your comfort zone. You are the most self-sacrificing person we know and you don't look out for your own needs. Ever."

"It's true," Courtney said. "Everything you do is in service of being a single mom. Never for you, as a woman. We thought that by you saying yes to everything, you might try some things that you'd end up liking. For you."

Lucy shook her head. "But it sounds like it backfired and just filled your plate too full."

Maybe that was exactly how it had gone. Thinking back, she had said yes to things she ended up liking. Nick was one of them. But her plate had definitely felt too full.

"My grandma Walker is staying here at my parents' house, too," Lucy said, "and I was talking to her yesterday. She said that after so many years of celebrating Christmas, one year she decided that it was all too much. So she sat down and decided what was most important to her to celebrate at Christmastime and pared everything way back. She said that she discovered that simple really was best. That all that mattered was the people you spent it with."

"Ooo, that's good," Courtney said. "Christmas doesn't have to be big to be special. Maybe you should take the day and kind of reevaluate what it is that's most important. You know, figure out what you want."

Maybe that was a really good idea. "Okay," she said. "I'll do it."

She ended the video call, and then said, "Aiden, I

need to work on my planner for a bit. Do you want to use your new paper and markers at the table with me while I do?" Since that was his favorite activity ever, she was able to sit down with him and really think.

She realized that over the years, she'd done every Christmassy thing with Aiden that came up because she grew up missing the entirety of every Christmas and didn't want Aiden to miss out on anything. So she let herself think about each thing they did and how much joy she thought it brought. She only put it on the list for next year if it truly felt integral to feeling the Christmas spirit. Then she asked Aiden what his two most favorite things to do at Christmastime were.

He said, "Making snowflakes, and..." He tapped the end of his marker against his lips. "I don't know. It's a toss-up between the hay ride and Christmas Eve."

Those were things that had landed on her list, too. She put stars by them to make sure they happened next year, but she was going to work hard to not feel like she had to do anything beyond that next Christmas unless they wanted to. She was going to spend it enjoying the people she loved.

She glanced at the window that showed her small backyard and noticed a few flakes of snow falling as the sun was setting. Last night didn't only happen because of her full schedule, though. She thought about what Courtney and Lucy said about wanting her to say yes to things so she'd find out what she really liked.

So she turned to a blank page in her planner and started writing down all the things she liked about Nick.

I love that he's a good dad.

I love that he loves Christmas.

I love that he makes everything fun.

I love how much he shows that he appreciates me.

I love the way he looks at me when he's listening to me talk about anything.

I love the way he makes me feel.

I love how he's willing to take on projects he's never done before and just assumes he can do it.

I love the color of his eyes. The way his hair has the perfect amount of curl. The way he looks in a t-shirt. Actually, the way he looks in everything.

I love his problem-solving, creative, thoughtful mind.

I love how much he loves his daughter.

I love how he talks about Clara with such respect and that their relationship was so great that her parents would still claim him as their son. I love that it

*gives me confidence that he'll always
treat me with respect, too.*

*I love how willing he was to do our
Christmas traditions, like cutting and
hanging snowflakes.*

*I love how I can talk to him for hours and
never run out of things to say.*

*I love how much he can make me laugh
with just a text.*

*I love how hard he worked to make his
house a home and how important that
was to him.*

*I love how safe and cherished I feel when his
arms are around me.*

I love how great a kisser he is.

Before long, every inch of the page was filled, even
the margins. Sometime in the past week or so, she'd
started focusing on what the relationship was doing to
her planned-out and ordinary schedule. But as she
worked on the list, she realized how much beauty and
depth a relationship with Nick brought to her life and
how much she had loved shouldering everything
together.

Her friends had pointed out that she never did
anything for herself and wanted her to figure out what
she wanted. She, Rachel, had her very own wants and

needs. And she was starting to understand what those were. Beyond how awful she'd felt after ending things, making the list helped her to realize that what she most wanted was a relationship with this man who she had spent this season falling in love with.

She looked over at Aiden, who was biting his top lip as he was cutting a snowflake out of a piece of paper that he'd decorated with his markers, and said, "You really like Nick, don't you?"

"Yeah."

"I really do, too. Do you want to help me think of something we can do to get him back in our lives?"

Aiden put his snowflake and scissors down and swung his legs around to kneel on the chair, leaning forward with his elbows on the table. "Yeah! Like what kind of something?"

"I don't know. We can brainstorm. Maybe something with a lot of helium balloons, or building two snowmen holding hands and then spelling out something in the snow. Or... making him giant gingerbread cookies. Oh! Maybe we could decorate that cute tree in his front yard with some kind of decorations that would, I don't know..."

Aiden was looking at her with his head cocked, his eyebrows drawn together.

"What?"

"Why does it have to be something big like that?

Holly said her dad has a picture of you from your date and he looks at it all the time when he doesn't know she's paying attention. She said he talks about you a lot, too. I think he really likes you. Can't we just go over there and you say, 'Hey I really like you, too. Let's go on dates again'?"

She just stared at Aiden. He had this simplicity thing down. Why *couldn't* it be that simple? "Aiden," she said, "you're brilliant." She kissed him on his forehead. "Go get your coat and gloves and hat. Let's go over to his house."

Aiden got his winter gear on in record time, he was so excited. Bailey was so excited. Rachel was so excited. The three of them piled into her car, and she pulled out of her driveway.

eighteen

NICK

"YOU'VE GOT YOUR COAT, hat, and gloves?" Nick asked as he grabbed his keys and the bag he'd filled and opened the door leading to the garage.

"Check, check, and check," Holly said. "But not check on my other shoe."

She hopped on one foot toward the door as she put her shoe on the other foot, then he, Holly, and Rosy all went into the garage, hopped into the car, and put their seatbelts on. He pushed the button hooked to his visor to open the big garage door at the same time he started the car. He looked into the rearview mirror as the door raised, but saw lights turning onto his driveway. Squinting at the brightness, he tried to make out whose car it was.

"Huh," he said. "I think Rachel is here."

Confused, he turned off his car and they all got out, meeting Rachel, Aiden, and her dog in his driveway. "What are you doing here?"

Rachel looked a bit... sheepish, was it? "I came to talk to you. But you're just leaving— I'm sorry. Do you need to go?"

He shook his head. "I was coming to talk to you." Did he dare hope that she wouldn't have shown up at his house today unless she had been every bit as unsettled as he was about how they'd left everything?

"You were?"

He nodded. "I wanted to tell you that I think I might have made a mistake."

"Yeah? I made a mistake, too. A really big one."

Hope started to fill him more. "Was your mistake in ending things? Because if it wasn't, this conversation is going to get awkward very quickly."

She chuckled softly. That was good. Right? "I might have freaked out because of my planner."

He nodded. "I got freaked out because of my deceased wife."

"Okay, you win."

"I guess I didn't have things figured out because dating again is so new. But then my father-in-law shared a lot with me that I needed to hear—things I hadn't considered that made me look at our relation- ship in a different light. And I realized that I didn't need to be freaking out about the things I was freaking out about."

"Aww," Rachel said. "Tell your father-in-law I think he's pretty great."

He definitely would. He needed to thank the man for himself again, too. "What about you?"

"Some friends set me straight. Aiden helped, too."

"Tell Aiden I think he's pretty great."

"Don't worry," Aiden said from where he and Holly stood half a dozen feet away. "I heard. Does this mean that you two are going to start dating again?"

Both he and Rachel chuckled, then looked at each other again. She was so beautiful, her dark hair falling in waves just below her red knit cap. The snow was coming down in big chunks, landing on the cap and her hair. He couldn't believe he almost let fear keep him from this woman, and he was so grateful that she was willing to talk about making things work.

"I would like to," he said. "What do you think? And don't feel obligated to say yes, even though it's still your Season of Yes."

She smiled and stepped closer to him. Their coats were brushing, their faces close enough that he could feel her warm breaths. "I would like to, also. Season of Yes or not."

"Yes!" Aiden and Holly both said, giving each other high-fives. It suddenly made him wonder how much matchmaking behind the scenes the kids had done that he hadn't known about.

"Can us seeing each other again start today? Because it feels like it's been a million years since I last saw you, and this heart of mine has been going through some serious withdrawals."

She smiled up at him. "Mine, too. And we can definitely start today."

He had thought once at the beginning of their relationship that it felt like he had jumped out of a plane. This moment felt like their parachutes had safely deployed and they were landing more or less gently on the ground.

Holly and Aiden ran off to play in the snow in their front yard as more fell from the sky. He reached out to brush a snowflake from Rachel's cheek. "So I won Aiden over, huh?"

"Yeah, but that was mostly because you showed him all the tools at The Home Improvement Store, and to a kid like Aiden, you opened up his mind to crafts on a much bigger scale." She chuckled. "In all seriousness, though. You totally won him over. All the way. I think you won us all over."

Bailey, the good girl that she was, took that moment to come over and sit at his feet, looking up at him like she just knew he was about to tell her how great she was.

"See?" Rachel said. "You even won Bailey over."

He reached down and rubbed the sides of Bailey's golden neck. "You really are a good girl."

When he stood straight again, Rachel nestled into his side, so he wrapped an arm around her shoulders, pulling her in close to keep her warm. And then they just stood there, snuggled together, watching their kids and their dogs playing in the snow, laughing, and throwing snow up into the air. He couldn't imagine a more perfect moment.

The night was cold enough to see their breath coming out in little cloud puffs, but with the low clouds, it wasn't a bitter cold. The moon was only a sliver tonight, but it still shone brightly, lighting the snow that softly fell from the sky and reflecting off all the snow on the ground, making the night seem brighter than it was.

He kissed Rachel on the temple. "You're pretty great, you know that?"

She shook her head. "Nope."

He didn't know if she meant that she didn't know or if she just wanted to hear more. Either way, he wanted to tell her how great he thought she was every day for the rest of her life. "Well, then, I better tell you."

She turned so that she was facing him, and he wrapped both arms around her waist. "I love that you're willing to try new things. I love that you're always on top of everything. That you look out for everyone's feelings.

That you always make Holly feel important and special. I love that you make a schedule. And that your purse is divided into sections."

Rachel looked down and laughed. Then she met his eyes again.

He continued. They were all coming to his mind so quickly that he couldn't stop. "I love that you make me feel like I can accomplish anything. I love the way your lips quirk up—like right now—when you're amused. I love how patient and understanding you are. I love that you've invited me and Holly into your life and that you've just as easily stepped into ours.

"I love that you're understanding about my relationship with Holly's grandparents and about Clara. I love that you bring so much joy to everything. I love that you make a point of celebrating things. People don't do that often enough and I think it's important. I love that you work hard and prioritize. And I love how you make me feel like I've come home."

The whole time, she just gazed at him like she was soaking it all in. When he finished, she said, "I am speechless. Thank you."

And then she rose on her toes and pressed her lips against his, sliding her arms around his neck, pulling them as close together as they could be in thick winter coats. Her kiss felt like a dream. Like a promise. A hope for the future.

When he'd pulled into this driveway the day he and Holly had moved to Mountain Springs, he never imagined he would be standing here on Christmas night, being so utterly and completely in love with someone he hadn't even met then. He knew that Christmas was a magical time of year, but being there with Rachel showed just how magical it could be.

He wanted to spend a lot more time kissing Rachel, but not in front of the kids, and not outside in the cold. He planted one last kiss on Rachel's lips, and then looked at the kids and dogs, who were starting to get cold.

"Should we go inside?"

Rachel nodded. "Then I can tell you all the things I love about you."

For as awful as the day had started, the ending couldn't be any better. He said, "Come on, kids," as he grabbed the bag from the passenger's seat. "Let's go inside and warm up."

"What's that?" Aiden asked, pointing at the bag.

"We decided," Holly said, "well, my dad decided but I helped, that since our parents met working on a fireplace and fell in love on that hay ride with the hot chocolate at Jack and Noelle's wedding that he should try to woo your mom with hot chocolate by the real fireplace."

Rachel's eyebrow rose as a smile played across her

lips. He should've known that Holly would tell everything.

"You fell in love with me on the hay ride?"

"And a million times since. What do you think? Should we go inside where it's warm and I can properly woo you?"

She smiled. "I'd like that."

nineteen

RACHEL

RACHEL WOULD ACCEPT Nick's wooing any day of the week. It didn't take long for Holly and Aiden to run off to see and play with Holly's Christmas presents. Rachel took the moment alone as an opportunity to tell Nick all the things she loved about him.

When she said the first thing, he placed a gentle kiss on her hand. When she said the second thing, he moved up about an inch and placed the next one. She told him everything that she could remember from her list, and he placed a kiss on her arm with each one. She even came up with new ones, because she wanted him to make it up to her neck before he stopped. With each kiss, it sent more and more tingles up her arm and so much dopamine to her brain that she could barely think.

When the kids and the dogs came back into the kitchen, dining room, and family room area, racing around and being crazy, Nick brought everyone together to play Outfoxed, a board game that they'd gotten for Christmas. Playing the cooperative clue game together was so much fun. Aiden and Holly actually worked together to solve the mystery instead of working in competition against each other. That, in itself, was a miracle.

Once the game was over, Nick left her side to go make hot chocolate for everyone while they put the pieces back into the box. He set Aiden's and Holly's mugs down on the table, where they were getting out a new game to play. When he came back with his and Rachel's mug, he nodded his head toward the couch, an eyebrow raised in question.

So they both went to the couch and she curled up next to him, the fire crackling in the fireplace, and he handed her a cup of hot chocolate. She wrapped her hands around the warm mug and inhaled. Her eyes went wide. "Is that cinnamon and ginger I smell? I can't believe you remembered that!" It was what she had put in her hot chocolate in the Allreds' yard, right before they got on the hay ride.

"Well, it was the day I fell in love with you, you know." He winked, and it did something to her heart.

She took a sip of it and savored the feel of the warm sweet chocolate and the taste of the spices on her tongue and knew that she would forever connect that taste with Nick falling in love with her.

Both dogs had followed them into the family room area and curled up just under the Christmas tree. The last time she'd been enjoying this fire with Nick, this house had been empty except for the fake fireplace that they had created. Now, the place was finished, furnished, and so inviting.

She snuggled into him even more, and he put an arm around her shoulders. Everything about this evening felt perfect. It was like all that had been missing this morning when it was just her and Aiden and cinnamon rolls was finally righted. It was all here.

Rachel placed her mug of hot chocolate on the coffee table and was resting her head against Nick's shoulder, watching the fire, when Aiden came and stood just in front of Nick, his coat in one hand. "I brought something." He reached into the pocket of his coat and pulled the object out. He let his coat drop to the floor and cradled it in both of his hands.

He stepped closer and showed them what he held. It was one of the doves from their tree. One of the ones that Aiden spent so much time running his fingers across every Christmas.

"It's a dove. It's got a little clip here instead of feet so you can clip it to a branch of your Christmas tree. Doves bring peace and happiness and they can even grant wishes!" Aiden shot a quick look at Rachel, almost like he was checking to see if she remembered that the wish he'd given to the dove in the park was for a new dad. "Can I put this one on your tree?"

Nick nodded. "I'd really like that."

Aiden carefully clipped the dove onto a branch of Nick's tree, then ran his finger along its back a couple of times, petting it. He turned and smiled at both of them before running back to the table to rejoin Holly in whatever game they were playing.

They both just looked at the bird for a long moment. Christmas really was about the people you spent it with and not about everything that was on—or not on—her planner. She couldn't believe she hadn't understood that before. She looked back at Nick. "For as long as I've gone without a man in my life, I now know that I never want to go without you again."

Nick smiled. "I came to the same conclusion."

"So what happens if one of us freaks out again and lets fear rule things a bit? I doubt we've gotten over the only hurdle we'll face."

"Well, we apparently know people we can go to for great advice." He chuckled softly, and she felt the rumble of it in his chest. "But mostly, I think we should go to each other first. Because I don't want this to ever end."

"I don't, either."

Nick's smile spread across his face gloriously, and he hadn't fully stopped smiling when his lips met hers for a kiss. She got it—she could barely stop smiling long enough to kiss him, too.

epilogue

NICK

NICK STROLLED DOWN Main Street with his gloved hand in Rachel's as they took in both the new and repeating Christmas decorations and lights all the shops had set up in their windows and in front of their buildings. It was the one-year anniversary of their first date, and they decided to recreate their date from a year ago.

They'd gone to the same restaurant. Last year, he'd just moved to Mountain Springs and had gotten the recommendation from his in-laws. Mountain Springs didn't have super fancy restaurants, but it was a nice one, the food was delicious, and the wait staff was so friendly. They'd gone several times since then, but tonight, they'd both ordered the same things they'd ordered on that first date.

Not only was it the anniversary of their first date, but it was their three-month wedding anniversary, so everything just felt extra great. This time, though, Jack and Noelle were the ones watching Holly and Aiden, and they were all at the home that Nick now shared with Rachel. He hadn't guessed when he bought the house that he'd find love again and be married to her less than a year later—he'd only known that the house had felt perfect from the moment he'd first stepped inside.

He hadn't known that it would be perfect beyond his imagination once Rachel became his wife and she and Aiden (and Bailey!) moved in. They had started the process for him to adopt Aiden and Rachel to adopt Holly the moment they got home from their honeymoon and it wouldn't be long before everything was officially official.

"I'm pretty proud of us," Rachel said.

"Oh, yeah?"

"We've done an excellent job making deliberate choices about Christmas activities this year."

Nick nodded in agreement. "I take it you've felt good about our Monthly Plan?"

"I do. It hasn't seemed like any of us have gotten overwhelmed and we've had tons of time to spend together as a family."

"Just the way I like it." He placed a kiss on Rachel's temple.

Rachel leaned her head against his shoulder as they walked, looking up at the lights that were strung from one side of the street to the other, taking in how nice everything looked.

Rachel stopped, still looking up. "I just felt a snowflake. I think it's starting to snow!" The look of joy on her face was something he would never tire of seeing in a million years.

They both stood still, watching as a meandering flake here and there made their way to the ground. And then a few more flakes started to fall. Before long, they were falling at a steady pace. Not that they didn't already have plenty of snow in their mountain town, but it always felt magical when new snow fell.

"I love that we are getting snow again, just like our date last year."

"I love that at the end of this one we won't have to go home to separate houses."

Rachel grinned up at him. "I like that, too." She cocked her head. "If we're repeating our date from a year ago... Do you think we'll get interrupted when we try to kiss this time?"

He chuckled. "I don't know. Our kids are a year older. And there aren't any big rocks hiding under the snow at our house for Holly to hurt her ankle on. But just to be on the safe side, we better kiss right now."

Rachel moved closer to him, but then said, "No, wait! We have to do our selfie first!"

He pulled out his phone, opened the camera, and flipped the screen to their faces. They were both smiling like a couple who had spent a year getting everything figured out and were loving where they were at. He snapped the picture, and then placed a soft kiss on her lips. "Happy anniversary, my wife."

"Happy anniversary, my husband."

The moment he grinned back at her, her phone rang. She pulled it from her coat pocket, said, "It's Jack," then answered the call and put it on speaker phone.

"It's time," Jack said, a note of excitement and worry in his voice.

"Noelle is in labor? Okay, we'll—"

"No, not Noelle. Everything is totally fine with her. It's time for *Bailey*. Her first puppy is already here!"

"She's early!" Rachel said. "The vet said it wouldn't happen until next week!"

"Well, I don't think that the babies heard that bit of news, because they are coming now. Remember how she didn't come running to us when we showed up? Apparently, she was hiding in the room you got ready, nesting around the box and blankets you'd set up."

Rachel turned and started walking in the direction of their car, which was parked a couple of blocks away. "I need to call the vet."

"That was the first call Noelle made," Jack said. "He's out of town—some emergency with his adult daughter. But don't worry—Noelle seems to know exactly what she's doing. And she said that more importantly, Bailey knows exactly what *she's* doing and we just need to monitor her and not interfere. So don't stress out and don't feel like you need to hurry. Everything is under control."

As he and Rachel hurried back down Main Street toward their car, talking about how they and Jack and Noelle had decided that they needed more golden retrievers in their lives, Rachel said, "If we recreate our first date every single year, do you think we'll always get an emergency call at this point in the date?"

He chuckled. "Let's hope not. But who knows? Fifty years from now, we might be walking down this path with our canes and get a call that one of our grandkids just got proposed to."

When they got home, they pulled into the garage and hurried into the house. He glanced around the kitchen, dining, and family room area that was even more decorated than it was last Christmas, snowflakes already hanging from the ceiling, just as Holly and Aiden came running toward them, their rough collie, Rosy, at their feet.

"Bailey is doing so good!" Holly said. "She hasn't needed any help at all."

Aiden nodded. "We didn't even know she was having her babies. We thought she was just tired from having that big belly and didn't want to play. But then I kept hearing weird sounds, and I found Bailey with a teeny baby puppy!"

They were trying to make their way to the small room off the kitchen that they'd just been using for storage until they cleared it out for Bailey when Holly held up a hand. "I'm going to warn you that it's gross in there."

"That's okay," Nick said.

They found Bailey in her whelping box, two little cream-colored puppies near her, their eyes closed, taking a couple of stumbling steps. Bailey's mouth was open in her signature smile, looking so proud of her babies. A very pregnant Noelle was sitting on the floor nearby, Jack at her side, and she smiled up at them like she was just as proud.

"Aren't they the cutest?" Aiden said from the doorway, where Rosy was turning around in circles with excitement. "I just want to pick one up in my hands and cuddle it."

"Soon, sweetie," Rachel said. "Right now, we're going to let Bailey enjoy them."

Two hours later, Bailey had given birth to the final puppy—number five—and they had gotten the area cleaned up, Bailey fed and resting peacefully with her babies. Not long after, they quietly said goodbye to Jack and Noelle, then read a Christmas bedtime story to Holly and Aiden before getting them tucked into bed.

Then they went back to check on Bailey and her puppies. They stood in the doorway, Rachel leaning against him as they took in the five sleeping puppies snuggled into Bailey. He put his arms around Rachel and pulled her close. They wouldn't be keeping all the puppies—they'd already promised one to Jack and Noelle and at least two to friends, but there still came with the puppies a feeling of their family expanding, just like it had when they'd joined their two little families together.

He soaked in the feeling, enjoying every moment of it. Then he kissed Rachel's temple and said, "I guess our schedule for the rest of December is going to be thrown off a bit."

"I hear that's not the most important part of the season. It's all about the people you spend it with." She twisted a bit to smile up at him. "Whatever life throws at us or our little family, we can handle."

He placed a kiss on her lips. "Yes, we can."

Author's Note:

I hope you enjoyed reading Rachel and Nick's love story! Writing the story of these two parents and the obstacles they faced on their way to their happily ever after kept me whistling *It's the Most Wonderful Time of the Year.* I hope it has left you smiling and maybe whistling a carol or two.

If you missed Noelle and Jack's in *The Christmas Pact*, you can get it here. Katie, the youngest Allred is getting her own story coming Christmas of 2023. You can sign up for my newsletter here so you don't miss a release!

—Meg

Want to read more Christmas romances by Meg Easton?

Get *Stockings, Snow, and Mistletoe* —two full-length Christmas romances to snuggle up with and swoon over. Both are full of heart, humor, hope, and all the magic of Christmas wrapped up in one holiday-filled collection.

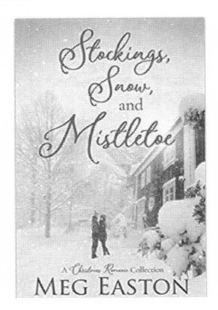

more small-town romance from meg easton

Second Chance on the Corner of Main Street
Christmas at the End of Main Street
More than Friends in the Middle of Main Street
Love Again at the Heart of Main Street
More than Enemies on the Bridge of Main Street
Coming Home to the Top of Main Street

more titles from meg

How to Not Fall for the Guy Next Door
How to Not Fall for the Wrong Guy
How to Not Fall for Your Best Friend
How to Not Fall for Your Ex

about meg

Meg Easton writes contemporary sweet and clean romance. She lives at the foot of a mountain with her name on it (or at least one letter of her name) in Utah. She loves gardening, bike riding, baking, swimming before the sun rises, and spending time with her husband and three kids.

She can be found online at www.megeaston.com, where you can sign up to receive her newsletter and stay up to date with new releases, get exclusive bonus content, and more.

If you liked this book please leave a review. Your review can help other readers find books they might fall in love with.

 facebook.com/MegEastonBooks